THE FORTRESS
OF KASPAR SNIT

Cary Fagan

Tundra Books

Published in Canada by Tundra Books,
481 University Avenue, Toronto, Ontario M5G 2E9

Published in the United States by Tundra Books of Northern New York,
P.O. Box 1030, Plattsburgh, New York 12901

Library of Congress Control Number: 2003112179

Library and Archives Canada Cataloguing in Publication

Fagan, Cary
   The fortress of Kaspar Snit / Cary Fagan.

For children aged 8-12.
ISBN 0-88776-665-X

   I. Title.

PS8561.A375F67 2004   JC813'.54   C2003-905209-5

We acknowledge the financial support of the Government of Canada
through the Book Publishing Industry Development Program
(BPIDP) and that of the Government of Ontario through the
Ontario Media Development Corporation, Ontario Book Initiative.
We further acknowledge the support of the Canada Council for the
Arts and the Ontario Arts Council for our publishing program.

Design: Terri Nimmo

Printed and bound in Canada

4 5 6   09 08 07 06 05

To Michael, Daniel, and Barbara

THE FORTRESS
OF KASPAR SNIT

1

THE

UNDERPANTS PETITION

We were in the middle of dinner when I said, "Why can't I learn to fly?"

My mother had been raising a forkful of lasagna to her mouth, but she stopped to give me the look. You know that look – the one that parents give when you've asked for something once too often.

I guess my father didn't hear – he was always thinking of something else – because he said, "I got a very interesting offer today. There's a fountain in Istanbul, eight hundred years old, hasn't worked for centuries. The Turkish government wants me to advise them on how to restore it. The water source comes from a stream. . . ."

"If Eleanor gets to learn to fly, then I want to learn too," said Solly. His name was Saul, but everybody called him

Solly. Maybe when he was older he wouldn't let anyone call him Solly anymore, but right now he was seven years old and a shrimp. Actually, he never called himself Saul *or* Solly. Not at home. Not at school. Not at the park. Not anywhere, ever. He always called himself Googoo-man. In my opinion, it was the most ridiculous name for a super-hero ever imagined. But it came about because *goo-goo* was the first sound Solly ever made and, somehow, it stuck in that pea-sized brain of his.

As always, Solly had come to dinner dressed in his Googoo-man superhero outfit. Green stretchy pajamas with a red bathing suit pulled over it. A cape made from a bath towel with the words PROPERTY OF HOTEL SCHMUTZ printed on it. Swim goggles and rubber bathing cap with chin strap. Swim flippers. Belt made from a thousand elastic bands tied together. Two weapons tucked into the belt: a "sonic blaster" (bicycle horn) and a "neutronic knocker" (old sock filled with unidentifiable substance). Would *you* trust a seven-year-old kid dressed this way to save the world?

"You're too young to fly," I snapped, "just a kid. You can have fun pretending, like you always do. But I'm too old to pretend. I'm old enough –"

"You're *both* kids," my mother said wearily. "And for the hundredth time, no, Eleanor, you can't learn to fly."

"What's that?" my father said, blinking. "Eleanor, are you starting up again? You know your mother's and my attitude about that. There will be no children learning to fly in this house."

2

"But it isn't fair!" I insisted. "I really am old enough. I have lots of responsibilities now. I have to walk Solly to school. I have to make my bed. I have to clear the table. Why can't I have any *fun* responsibilities? What's the use of being eleven if I can never do anything I want?"

"You get to do lots of things that you want," Mom said, trying to sound understanding. "You went to a movie with your friends last week, didn't you? Your father is a grown-up and he doesn't fly."

"That's because he doesn't want to. But I do."

My mother looked at my father and raised her eyebrows. She knew it was true. But my father shook his head. "Listen, Eleanor," he said, "I know how tempting it must seem. But your mother and I agreed before we even got married – didn't we, Daisy? – that there would be no more flying in her family. Mom would be the last one. We want you and Solly to be normal, everyday children enjoying normal, everyday things. We want you to be just like everybody else. And being able to fly isn't exactly like everybody else, is it?" My father flicked out his arm to uncover his watch from under his shirt cuff. "See? It's getting late. The fountain turn-off ceremony is supposed to be in ten minutes."

"I don't feel like going to the ceremony," I said.

"Of course you do." My father smiled. "It's a family tradition."

My mother looked at me sympathetically. "Maybe we should excuse Eleanor just tonight, Manfred."

"Never mind," I said. "I'll come to the dumb ceremony. And by the way, Dad, there's nothing normal about a

3

fountain turn-off ceremony. I mean, do you see anybody else on the street having one?"

"That's different," Dad said. "It's still in the realm of regular human behavior. It doesn't require any – well, any special powers. There's nothing freakish about it."

"Manfred!" Mom cried. "Do you think I'm a freak?"

"Of course not." Dad put his hand on his high forehead. "This conversation never ends well."

"But flying would be so cool," I said, even though I knew it was a lost cause. "Nobody would have to know about it. I'd keep it a secret. Solly would keep it a secret too, wouldn't you, Solly?"

Solly just looked at me and grinned, his mouth full of lasagna. A big help he was. I turned back to my parents. "A fountain is definitely not cool. A fountain – especially *our* fountain – is embarrassing."

"That's enough, Eleanor Galinski Blande," Mom said.

"It's time," Dad said, putting down his napkin and pushing away from the table.

A couple of years ago, my mother gave me a book called *The Big Orange Splot* by Daniel Pinkwater (I swear that's his real name). In this book a man decides to paint his house all kinds of crazy colors. At first the neighbors don't like it, but then each neighbor gets inspired to decorate his own house just the way he likes it. Mom gave me this book to help me understand what Dad did to our house. I think she hoped that, after reading the book, I wouldn't be so embarrassed.

Well, I read the book, and I was still embarrassed. The reason was simple: none of the other families on *our* street changed their houses. They stayed just as they were before – regular houses, each with a garage and a square of grass and a little flower bed and a spindly tree. I guess our neighbors never got the message.

Actually, there was nothing strange about our house itself. It looked just like the bungalow three doors down and the one three doors up. It was what was in front of our house that was different. The reason that the four of us now marched single file, Solly's flippers making flopping noises, out the front door and onto the sidewalk.

A fountain.

A fountain? Not so bad, you might think. *Fountains are kind of nice, aren't they?* But this was a big fountain. A very big fountain. A *monumentally* big fountain.

As we stood on the sidewalk I was struck, as always, by how it filled our entire front yard, right to the sidewalk's edge. It began with a big square basin, with marble sides that rose as high as my waist. The basin held a pool of water: ten thousand gallons, to be precise. Out of the middle rose eight winged horses, carved out of marble and larger than life. The horses reared up on their hind legs, heads held high, eyes wild, nostrils flaring. On the back of each horse was a man or a woman (four of each) holding a conch shell, out of which spouted jets of water that splashed down to the basin. The men were very handsome and the women beautiful, with sculpted faces that looked alive and flowing marble hair and magnificently formed arms and legs.

They were also totally naked.

Which meant that we had four naked women and four naked men on our front lawn. That added up to eight butts. It was well known in the neighborhood that the first naked people little kids around here ever saw (besides their own family) were the statues of our fountain. They discovered what people look like without clothes on by *staring* at our fountain. Mothers were always pulling their open-mouthed kids away from the sidewalk in front of our house. Once, around dinnertime, I caught a teenaged boy gazing at the second woman on the right. I swear he looked like he had fallen in love with her. I opened the front door and shouted, "Move it, buster! What do you think this is, health education class?" Boy, did he take off.

After we were properly lined up, my father took two steps forward. He opened a little door in the side of the basin that was invisible unless you knew where to look. Inside the tiny compartment was a small wheel-like tap and, as my father now turned it, the streams of water shooting from the conch shells slumped lower and lower until they became just a drip. Without the sound of the falling water, everything turned quiet. My father patted the side of the fountain and my mother said, "All right, everybody, back inside."

As we filed in again, I noticed our next-door neighbor Mr. Worthington, along with his children Jeremy and Julia, watching us through the parted curtains of their front window. Mr. Worthington had once taken a petition up and down the street. He knocked on every door wearing his bowler hat, and with his umbrella on his arm. The petition demanded that my father put underpants and T-shirts on the statues. *In defense of public decency*, it said. After he got a whole sheet of signatures, Mr. Worthington knocked on our door and solemnly presented the petition to my father. Dad read it over and, thinking that Mr. Worthington was making a joke, laughed so hard that he couldn't breathe. He had to lie down right in the front hall. Mr. Worthington just looked at my father until finally he put his bowler hat back on and returned to his own house.

But after that, my father did start the fountain turn-off ceremony. It's surprising how noisy all that whooshing water can be and my father decided that, while he found the sound very soothing, not all the neighbors likely appreciated it. He turned it on again at precisely 6:45 A.M., but he didn't expect us to get up and watch. Sometimes I came out anyway and, when my father turned the tap, there would be a little spurt from each conch shell, then a bigger spurt, and finally a gusher. At that moment all the neighborhood dogs would howl.

We began filing back into the house, with my father at the front and me coming up the rear. I felt a tap on my shoulder and turned around to see Julia Worthington standing on the sidewalk behind me. She was wearing her leotard, her hair pulled back in a bun.

"Hi, Eleanor," she said.

"Hi, Julia."

"Doing that crazy fountain thing, huh?" She made a goofy face, crossing her eyes and twisting her mouth to one side.

"I guess so," I said.

"I just learned how to do a triple back flip. I'm going to do it in my freestyle program for the June finals. You want to see it?"

No, I didn't want to see Julia Worthington do a stupid back flip. But I didn't have the courage or the guts or whatever it took to say so and just nodded instead. She stepped onto her own lawn – unlike ours, it had actual grass – and before I could blink, she was flipping backwards in the air, landing on her hands, and flipping again. The sour truth is, I was hoping she'd crash onto her rear end but she didn't and, when she came up after the third time, she had a smile fixed on her face like she was trying to impress a jury of Olympic judges.

"That's . . . that's great, Julia."

"Thanks. Well, I've got to go. I have to practise the harp now. I'm learning a new Mozart piece."

She gave a little wave and ran up her porch stairs. That was another thing about Julia. She couldn't play the piano or the trumpet like everybody else. She had to play the harp. She played at every school assembly, her hands running across all those harp strings to make a sound like a musical waterfall. Julia never did anything that anybody else did – unless she could do it better. It was weird, considering how much I didn't like her (although I wasn't even sure if it was fair that I didn't like her), that I still wished she would be my friend. I stood alone on the side-walk a minute and then I trudged back into the house.

In the night, I woke up and couldn't get back to sleep. I listened to the sound of Solly in the next room, whistling through his teeth while he slept. The chair at my desk cast a long shadow against the wall that looked like the bars of a cage. It felt as if, even before I woke up, I'd been thinking about my friends at school, especially Julia Worthington. Everyone liked Julia and I didn't think that I'd ever seen her alone at school. She always had one or two girlfriends with her in the hall, or the washroom, or at recess. I mean, it wasn't like I was some friendless loner exactly, but I always felt on the edge of things, as if it didn't really make a difference whether I was sitting with the other girls at lunch or going along to the movie. There wasn't anything special about me, anything to make them really, really like me.

I made myself close my eyes, but I knew that I wouldn't be able to go back to sleep right away so I got up and went over to the window. In the dark I could see the shape of our swing and teeter-totter set that I used to love so much when I was little. Over the back fence were the roofs of other houses and a couple of old TV antennas, even though people didn't use them anymore. Two or three stars in the sky. And then, above the trees and maybe four or five streets away, I saw my mother moving through the night sky – the wind blowing back her hair, her hands near her sides, and her toes pointed back. So she was flying tonight. How I wished that I knew how she did it! How I wished

that I could fly too! It seemed to me that just about everything would be better if I could. I watched as my mother
rose higher and veered away, disappearing behind the rise
of trees from the neighborhood park. It wasn't fair that
she wouldn't teach me, that I had to be just like regular
kids when I wanted to be special too. Well, maybe if she
wouldn't teach me, I would have to find out for myself.
After all, that's what Mom did.

Determined now, I climbed back into bed.

2

A BRIEF
HISTORY OF FLIGHT

It was because of Solly that I discovered my mother could fly. One night, about six months earlier, he had woken me up by talking in his sleep. "*I laugh in the face of danger! Unhand her, you scoundrel! I won't rest until you are behind bars!*"

I got up and went into his room to see that Solly had half slipped out of bed. His head and arms dangled upside down over the side, while one leg stuck straight up like a flagpole. Somehow he'd even managed to get his swim goggles hanging from his big toe. I took down the goggles and shoved him properly into bed.

"You can't push Googoo-man around," he muttered, and then buried his face in his pillow.

Coming out of Solly's room, I heard a noise. So I crept down the hall and, peering into the living room, saw my mother standing before an open window. A breeze ruffled the curtains. Although it was the middle of the night, my mother wore a T-shirt, sweatpants, and sneakers, like she was about to go for a midnight jog. She had her chin tilted up and her arms stretched behind her, and she kept rising on her toes and coming down again. Her face had a dreamy expression and a kind of half-smile. The breeze rustled her loose hair and I saw her lips move like she was saying something, and then she rose on her toes again and lifted off the ground – off the ground! – and up through the open window.

What the . . .?

At first I couldn't do anything except stare at the space where, a moment before, my mother had been standing. I went to the window, but I couldn't see anything except for the shadows of bushes and the swing set. Then looking higher up I caught sight of my mother above the trees, the moonlight turning her silvery. She kept her arms back, but didn't move her limbs – no flapping, or leg-kicking, or anything like that. It looked more like she was sailing through the air. She rose higher, so that I could see her pass over the roof of the school, and then she was out of sight.

Even though I couldn't see her anymore, I watched out the window for a while longer. Then I sat in a big armchair in the living room to wait. Strange though it was to discover that my mother could fly, I didn't feel really surprised. It was as if I had known all along that Mom could do some extraordinary thing. Her job always sounded boring to me – working in the local passport office, standing behind a window and taking people's applications. I had been to the office and it sure was dull. Just people sitting in stacking chairs waiting to be called, holding on to their numbers as if they were afraid of losing them. But once when I asked her how she could stand it, she said she enjoyed her work. "People tell me about the trips they're going to take, which is why they need their passports. I like listening and sharing in their anticipation. I suppose I don't need a very exciting job. Life is exciting enough."

"It is?" I had said to her. "What's so exciting about it?"

"Well, taking care of you and Solly for one thing."

But she hadn't fooled me. There was nothing exciting about taking care of us. And now I knew what the exciting thing was. Everything made sense – her faraway looks, why she was so tired on some mornings. Her occasional wistful comments to my father at breakfast, like "It rained over Paris last night," or "The Rocky Mountains are more snow-covered this year." I suppose flying was the reason she liked her job at the passport office. It gave her ideas about where to fly.

I must have dozed off waiting, for my eyes suddenly opened when I heard a soft thud in the room. And there was Mom, standing inside the window again, her eyes momentarily closed as she released her arms to her sides. Her hair was damp with early morning dew. I waited for her to open her eyes and turn her head and, when she saw me, a look of surprise came over her face. I don't know why but I jumped up and rushed to my room, closing the door and getting into bed, where I pulled the covers over me. Maybe it was because I didn't think flying was cool at first. I thought it was weird and, to use my father's word, freak-ish. I was afraid that Mom would come into my room and try to talk to me, but she didn't and I stayed under the covers until it was time for school.

The next morning I got dressed, but stayed in my room for as long as I could. Mom came by every five minutes to knock on the door and say in a voice straining to sound casual, "Eleanor, you're going to be late for school." Only at the last minute did I dash out, snatch a piece of toast from the plate on the kitchen table, bolt down half a glass of milk, and grab Solly's hand to whirl him out the door.

In school, I could hardly concentrate. I kept seeing my mother's dreamy expression as she lifted off her toes and through the open window. I looked at the kids around me – Julia Worthington was leaning over her math homework, her tongue sticking out of the corner of her mouth – and wondered what they would think if they knew. I felt very strange – exhilarated even – my heart beating fast. I kept thinking, *My mother, Daisy Galinski, can fly? That's just as it should be.*

After school on Tuesdays, Solly always went to his friend Ginger Hirshbein's to play, so I didn't have to take him home. Ginger was the perfect playmate for Solly since he had endless patience for being rescued by Googoo-man just as he was about to be flattened by Kaspar Snit's

Flattening Machine, or turned into soup by Kaspar Snit's Melting Machine, or made into toast by his Human Toaster. I, myself, headed for the school library instead.

Mrs. Mintoff, the librarian, was putting up a display on the front table. She had made a sign on the bulletin board above it with construction paper letters – DON'T READ THESE BOOKS – and now she was arranging the books on the table.

"Are they banning books again, Mrs. Mintoff?" I said. Our librarian was always getting in a huff when somebody tried to prevent kids or adults from reading some book. She said that people were smart enough to judge for themselves.

"No, not these, Eleanor," she said. "These are just good books. But if I put up a sign that says GOOD BOOKS, nobody will take them out. With this sign they'll all be gone by tomorrow."

She winked at me and got back to arranging them. I walked to the other end of the library, the resource section, and after making sure that nobody else was around, I sat cross-legged on the carpet and began to pull books from the shelf:

The Development of Air Travel
The Picture History of Flight
Aerodynamics Made Easy.

I flipped through their pages, skimming the information on lift, thrust, air resistance, wing shape, velocity. There was nothing about how a human being might close her eyes, set back her arms, and take off into the night sky.

A voice behind me said: "I'm not in those books, Eleanor."

It was my mother. She groaned as she plunked down next to me. I saw that she was still in her work clothes – a dull dress, eyeliner, hair pinned back. I could see little creases around her eyes and mouth as she smiled at me. I didn't know whether I felt like smiling back.

"How come you never told me you could . . . you know?"

"I have an idea," she said. "Why don't just the two of us go to the mall and have ourselves a giant order of fries. We can talk there. Okay?"

"Okay."

The Maple Forest Mall, a ten-minute drive, had to be the most boring mall in the universe. Of course there weren't any maple trees around it – they'd all been cut down. The clothes in the shops were boring, the ice-cream booth had dull flavors, even the kiddy rides were so unexciting that Solly refused to go on them. Mom and I headed for Champion Charlie's Chip Wagon, which wasn't a wagon at all but just one of the counters in the food court.

We sat at a plastic table with the chairs bolted to the floor, in case anyone might want to steal them. I put ketchup on the fries.

"So?" Mom said. "Don't you want to ask me anything?"

"I don't know where to start. Well, when did *you* start? I mean, when did you first ever fly?"

"I was still a kid."

"My age?"

"A little older. And just like you, I'd seen my mother. It was funny because I had dreamed about flying so many times."

"What does it feel like?"

"Let me think. Well, it's like skating and swooshing on a toboggan and bouncing on a trampoline and jumping off a dock into a lake, all at the same time. It makes you forget your troubles, your little worries, so that you just feel alive and free. That doesn't mean it's easy, though. In fact, I'm always exhausted when I get back, like I've run twenty miles. It takes a lot of energy."

"How come? I didn't see you moving. I mean, you're not waggling your arms or kicking your legs."

Mom laughed. "I know. But it takes a lot of energy anyway. I have to keep my muscles taut in just the right way. If I haven't flown for a while, the first time out again my arms and legs feel sore the next day, just like yours do after riding your bike for the first time in spring. Most of all, though, the energy needed is up here." Mom touched her forehead with a finger. "It takes special concentration. I have to be absolutely focused and yet relaxed at the same time. It's like clearing your mind of everything in the past and everything you hope or fear in the future so that you can be in that very moment only. I remember one time I flew, I lost my focus and fell."

"Did you get hurt?"

"Just some bruises and scrapes. Luckily I was only about fifteen feet up and fell into the Worthingtons' hydrangea bushes."

"And where do you go when you fly?"

"Sometimes just in the neighborhood. I look down at the dark squares of lawn, the strings of lights along the empty streets, the blue and red glow of store windows or movie theaters. You should see how beautiful things are at night from above. But sometimes I go farther. I can fly pretty fast if I get sufficient altitude and a wind at my heels. Niagara Falls lots of times. Montreal. Boy, you should see New York City at night – it's spectacular. I even went to Paris once, that weekend last summer when Dad took you and Solly camping. And I've gone the other way too, right across the country to the giant fir-tree forests of the West Coast. And the mountains! It's cold above those snowy peaks."

I thought about what it must be like to fly over all those places. I didn't say anything, but just dipped a fry in ketchup and munched it. Then I said, "So teach me, Mom. Teach me how to fly."

"I shouldn't have talked that way," she said, looking regretful. "I shouldn't have made it sound so good."

"It's too late. You've got to teach me."

"I can't."

"But why not?"

"Because your father and I agreed. It was hard enough telling him that I could fly, before we got married. I was afraid he would think I was too different, too, well . . ."

"Weird?"

"I guess so. And he did have a hard time at first. But he got used to the idea, more or less. Only we agreed that if we ever had kids, we would try and keep it a secret from them. And if they ever found out, I wouldn't show them how. We agreed – me and your Dad both – that it would be better for our kids to be just like everybody else."

"But what if I don't want to be like everybody else? What if I don't feel like everybody else already?"

"I know it sounds unfair, Eleanor, and I'm really sorry. But maybe one day you'll be glad. No, I won't teach you."

"I won't be glad. And hey, your mother taught *you* how to fly."

"Actually she didn't. And she wasn't very happy when I figured it out. Now I think we'd better go home. Dad and Solly will be wondering where we are."

And so that was that, at least until now. Maybe it took me six months of brooding to decide that I wanted to fly even if they didn't want me to. Why couldn't I make the decision for myself? Were my parents going to tell me I couldn't learn to drive when I got older, or go to university, or travel on the bus? And after all, my mother didn't obey her mother either, so she could hardly expect me to obey her.

And that was why, after everybody was asleep, and I could hear Solly once more whistling in the next room, and I checked to make sure that my mother wasn't going on a little trip of her own that night, I found myself standing in the living room before the open window. Since I didn't know exactly what to do, I decided that I'd better imitate my mother as closely as possible. I had even put on a T-shirt and sweatpants, only my shirt said CAMP HUTZPAH on it. Now I stretched back my arms, positioning my hands just as I'd seen my mother do, tilted up my chin, and closed my eyes. I tried to imagine lifting up in the air and I even rose up on my toes. I tried to think like a bird. I tried to feel lighter than air. I tried to think like an airline pilot. I made little jumps up and down.

Nothing.

I opened my eyes again. Something was missing, but what could it be? Maybe I had to say something under my breath, some magic word. Once more I closed my eyes, tilted up my chin, rose up on my toes.

"*Abracadabra.*"

Nope.

"*Sim sala bim.*"

Uh-uh.

Come on, Eleanor, you can do it. Fly, girl, fly. Up, up, and away. You've got the right stuff, you know you have. . . .

"What are you doing?"

I opened my eyes to see Solly rubbing his and staring at me. "Can't a person ever get any privacy around here?"

"Why are you trying to jump out the window?"

"Come on, Solly. I'll take you back to bed."

I put my hand on his shoulder and he dutifully turned around. Well, it wasn't working anyway. There was something I still didn't know, but I was determined to find out.

3

THE FILE

ON GOOGOO-MAN

At breakfast Solly looked tired. He had put his goggles on crookedly, which made him look more goofy than usual.

"What's wrong with you this morning, Solly?" Dad said. "Didn't you sleep last night?"

"I got up and saw El –"

Quickly I interrupted with, "I think you had a bad dream. *Right*, Solly?"

He looked at me.

"But you were standing at the window and –"

"You mean that you *dreamed* I was standing at the window and . . . and a monster was trying to come in. Right, Solly?"

"If you say so," he yawned. "I'll have a cappuccino."

Mom answered, "Little boys don't drink coffee."

"But Daddy's having a cappuccino."

"Your daddy likes to pretend he's living in Rome."

"Don't we live in Rome?"

"No," I said. "We live in a *typical North American suburb*, as my teacher Mr. Bentham calls it, which is about as far from Rome as you can get. And which reminds me, I have to do a presentation in class today. It's called My Parent's Job."

"Well, talk about your father, not me," Mom said. "My job's not very interesting."

Solly dutifully spooned his cereal into his mouth. "I'm sure I did see the window open last night," he said. Unfortunately, he was too far for me to kick under the table. "It must have been the evil Kaspar Snit trying to come in and steal my sonic blaster and neutronic knocker."

"Very funny," I said, faking a laugh. "He has such an imagination, our Solly. . . . About the window, I mean."

My dad just looked at me. Then he said, "Solly, you do know that Kaspar Snit is only make-believe, don't you?"

"If it makes you feel better to think so, Dad, go ahead."

My father shook his head. "I don't understand my children anymore. And I've got to get to work."

"Me too," said Mom, getting up.

"You mean, you don't understand us anymore either?" Solly said, grinning. "Well, maybe nobody really understands a superhero."

That afternoon I had to do my presentation for Mr. Bentham's class. Mr. Bentham liked to listen to our talks

22

while sitting on top of the filing cabinet, his bald head almost touching the ceiling. To get there he had to climb onto his own desk and then use one of the cabinet drawers as a step. But once up there, he seemed awfully happy – legs crossed, eyes half closed, the rubber end of a pencil rooting around in his ear.

Julia Worthington, sitting at the next desk, leaned over to me. "I just learned how to play a Beatles song on the harp," she said.

"Great," I said, although it accidently came out as a question – more like, "Great?"

"All right, Ms. Worthington," said Mr. Bentham from his high perch. "Why don't you start the class presentations today."

Julia told us about her father, who was an insurance adjuster. According to Julia, his job was to find a way not to pay people their insurance money when their houses burned down or their cars fell apart. Next, Emily Blurr told us about her mother, who worked for a deodorant company. Her job was to test new deodorants by sniffing people under the arms. It was the sort of day that made a kid think twice about wanting to grow up.

Listening, I tried to decide what to say about my own father's job. My dad was the world's foremost expert on fountains, which explained the spouting monument in our front yard. Where we lived there weren't a lot of fountains, and most of the ones around were pretty lame. In North America we don't have the tradition, my father said. That was why he went to Italy, to the city of Rome, to study.

Rome is famous for being the city of fountains and there is even a university program dedicated to studying them. That was just what my father wanted.

Of course, to travel to Italy you need a passport. And it was at the passport office, six months before his plane was to leave, that he met my mom. Well, the short story is that, just before leaving for Rome, they got married. Now my dad got calls from all over the world. If some king or queen or president wanted to build a new fountain, or fix an old one, he or she would call my father. When it came to fountains, he was the man.

Without opening his eyes or removing the end of the pencil from his ear, Mr. Bentham called on me next. I got up and stood before the class, but as everybody stared at me I remembered how embarrassed I was by our fountain and its eight naked butts. I opened my mouth, but no words came out.

"Eleanor?" said Mr. Bentham.

"*Um*, yes," I stumbled. "I'm going to talk about . . . my mother. She works in the passport office. . . ."

It was my job to walk Solly home from school at lunchtime and then again at the end of the day. Our house wasn't very far, just along the edge of the school field and then across the park to our street, but Solly had no sense of direction. Some days it seemed he could get lost going from the kitchen to the bathroom.

Usually as we walked, Solly yattered on while I kept

pretty much to myself, uselessly hoping that the other kids would think that the boy in the green pajamas, red bathing suit, cap, goggles, and flippers just happened to be walking beside me but was no actual relation. I would look at anything – a cat on a fence, a knocked-over garbage can – rather than look at Solly and give away our connection.

Today I was feeling even more resentful of having to walk with Solly. My parents thought I was old enough to be responsible for him, but not old enough to do anything I really wanted – anything really fun, or different, or special. I guess it was because of my brooding that I didn't notice that Solly wasn't yakking away as usual. In fact, he wasn't saying anything at all and, when I finally did look at him, I saw a very dejected little superhero, head hung down, flippers dragging with each step.

"What's wrong, Solly?"

"*Ah*, nothing."

"Come on, tell me."

"Jeremy Worthington was making fun of me." Jeremy Worthington was Julia Worthington's younger brother.

"Why was he making fun of you?" I asked.

"Because I get things backwards. When Mrs. Prickle asks me to spell a word out loud, I sometimes read the letters backwards. I don't do it on purpose. I'm discombobulated."

"You're not discombobulated," I said. "You're *dyslexic*. Mom says you're going to learn to read just fine. It's going to take a little longer, that's all."

"Some superhero I am."

"Oh, come on, Solly, you're a great superhero. Hey, tell you what. When we get home, we can make a file on Googoo-man."

Solly looked up at me through his goggles. "What's that?"

"You know, like in the comic books, where they list all the special powers and other essential information about a superhero. Like Superman's strength, or Spiderman's ability to climb walls."

"That's a great idea! Will you really help me do it?"

"Sure. Come on, let's go."

"Okay!"

The two of us ran home together, Solly with his PROPERTY OF HOTEL SCHMUTZ cape flapping behind him. That was the problem with resenting a younger brother; you always ended up having to be extra nice to him for some reason or other.

For this important project, I let Solly come into my room and even sit on my own bed. Then I put a new sheet of lined paper on my clipboard and we got started. This is what we came up with:

THE FILE ON GOOGOO-MAN

Superhero name: Googoo-man
Superhero age: Seven years old
Real identity: Saul (Solly) Blande, grade one student, Inkpotts Public School
Super weapons: Sonic blaster, neutronic knocker
Arch nemesis –

Here Solly interrupted me. "What's an arch nemesis?" he asked.

"That's your most notorious enemy, the one you're protecting the world from. You know, that guy you go on about."

"You mean, the evil Kaspar Snit?"

"That's the one."

We continued.

Arch nemesis: The evil Kaspar Snit
Enemy's hideout: Impenetrable fortress somewhere in the Verulian Mountains
Enemy's power: Warrior army
Enemy's goal: To deprive the world of beauty.

"Wait a second," I said to Solly. "Are you sure about that? Doesn't he want to turn everybody into slaves, or steal all the gold in the world, or maybe control the television stations? You know, like regular villains. Are you sure he wants to deprive the world of beauty?"

Solly shrugged. "Yup."

"Well, okay." I drew a line at the bottom of the page. "We're finished. Now you have a file, just like a real superhero."

"This is great," Solly said. "I'm going to put this up on my door. Thanks, Eleanor!"

He grabbed the sheet and rushed to his own room. Sometimes it was so easy to make a little brother happy; I wished it was as easy to make *me* happy. It was a good

thing that I stopped myself from adding three last entries
to the list:

*Number of extremely mortified sisters who wish their
brother wouldn't wear his pathetic superhero outfit
everywhere:* One
Sister's name: Eleanor Galinski Blande
Sister's superpowers: None.

4

BEHIND
THE TINY DOOR

So Solly was happy being Googoo-man, Dad was happy working on fountains, and Mom was happy taking her nightly flights to exotic places. But what about me? What did I have that made me feel special or different? That made life more than just a series of boring duties, like homework and drying the dishes after supper? Where was the special and talented *me*, Eleanor? Or maybe I was just Ordinary Eleanor, and it was no wonder that kids like Julia Worthington didn't pay much attention to me. Would *I* pay much attention to me?

These were the dreary thoughts I was having when I heard a noise. I was lying in bed, my hands behind my head, when I heard the distinct sound of the side door opening and closing again. I knew all the noises in our house and the side door had a peculiar soft muffled sound, not like the thud of the front door. I pushed off the covers, swung my feet onto the floor, and crept to the hall.

Nothing. The hall was dark, all the lights off still, including the one in my parents' bedroom. I moved as quietly as I could, avoiding the squeaky places in the floor, and stopped again at the living room entrance. The room was dark and empty. The same for the kitchen. Nobody had come in, which meant that somebody had gone out.

The side door was beside the kitchen, so I figured that I might get a clue by looking out the kitchen window. Carefully I peeped over the window ledge and sure enough I saw my mom, dressed in her T-shirt and sweatpants and sneakers, pressed up against the side of the garage. She looked like a spy in a thriller movie, or maybe an escaped prisoner of war trying to get past the guard towers. She peered all around – I ducked for a moment under the sill – and then stealthily made her way to the front of the house. After a few steps, I couldn't see her anymore.

Quickly I scurried into the dining room. I knelt under the window and lifted up the blind, just enough to see. Mom was creeping behind the quiet fountain, looking over to the Worthingtons' house and then the other way to make sure that no one was watching her. Then she crouched down and opened a tiny door in the lip of the fountain's basin.

A tiny door? Of course I knew that there was a door at the side, where my father turned the water on and off every day. But another at the back? What was it doing there and why didn't I know about it? My eyes opened wide as I watched my mother put her hand into the compartment and take something out. She held it up, dangling from a chain, and it glinted darkly. Then she put it in one hand and closed her fingers around it.

Just at that moment, there was another sound from inside the house. Again I knew it instantly – my father's slippered footsteps coming along the hall. There was no time for me to move and I was sure he would catch me, but he didn't come into the dining room, turning to the front door instead. A moment later I heard the door open.

"Daisy?"

Looking out the window, I saw my mother quickly put whatever it was back in the compartment and close the door.

"I'm here, Manfred," she whispered.

"What are you doing?"

"Just checking."

"Won't you come back inside? You need to sleep."

"All right."

She got up and came in through the front door, and I heard them both go down the hall and into their room, closing the door behind them. *Whew*, that had been close. But I sure wasn't going back to bed. I needed to know what was in that compartment. Of course, I couldn't move right away; I had to wait awhile to be sure that my parents were sleeping. But when I couldn't hold myself back a moment longer, I crept over to the front door, opened it as quietly as possible, and closed it behind me.

Night. I stood in my pajamas, in bare feet, and felt the cool spring air. I heard a rustle in a nearby tree – a bird or squirrel settling in its sleep – and then silence. In one quick leap I was at the fountain, crouching down as my mother had and feeling along the lip of the basin for the door. At first I felt nothing, but then, after going over the same place several times, I felt it on the tips of my fingers – the slightest indentation. Yes, it went up, across, down, and across again in a square. How did it open? There was no knob or latch. Then I had the idea of giving the door a gentle push in and, when I let go, the door sprung lightly open.

The compartment was really just a small square space cut in the stone, but on it lay something that looked like a necklace. Carefully I picked it up and held it out as my mother had, letting it dangle from the silver chain. It was also silver, very old and rubbed smooth and flat. It was a crooked rectangle shape and the word "amulet" came to mind, like something from an ancient book. I held it up close and was disappointed to see that it was blank – no jewels or decoration. But then I turned it around.

On the other side were some markings in raised silver. I felt them first with my fingers and then, once again, held the amulet close up to my eyes. I could just see the shape of a quarter moon and three stars in an arc facing the moon. The amulet was simple and yet very lovely, the way looking at the night sky itself sometimes feels, but as I was admiring it I heard something – like a garbage can being knocked over – and my heart jumped. Quickly I did just as

I had seen my mother do earlier, pressing the amulet against the palm of my hand. Then I put it back in the little compartment, closed the door so that it became invisible again, and scurried back to the front door. In another minute I was in my bed, blankets pulled up to my chin, feeling a strange warmth in my palm where the moon and stars had pressed into it.

The whole next day I felt odd; not sick exactly, but not myself either. My face was flushed and, sitting at my desk in Mr. Bentham's class silently doing my work, I felt my heart begin to race for no reason. At recess I sat with Julia Worthington and the other girls, all of whom were talking about some new television show they had watched the night before. I only pretended to listen and, when the girl beside me offered a bite of her donut, a wave of nausea ran through me.

My hand felt strange too. Hot and pulsing, as if I had burned it on the metal handle of a pot on the stove. When I had looked at it that morning, there seemed to be four tiny green marks. By lunchtime the marks had turned purple and had grown a little bigger. Looking at them, I felt a jolt of fear. What exactly had I done? Was something happening to me? Maybe this was some kind of punishment for disobeying my parents. I was starting to wish that I hadn't watched my mother, or found the amulet, or wanted to be anything but an absolutely dull and ordinary human being.

By late afternoon, I started to feel better. My face cooled down and the nausea disappeared. Sitting in our kitchen at dinnertime, I found myself ravenously hungry and asked for three helpings of spaghetti, so that my father asked if I had run a marathon this afternoon. Maybe my feeling sick had been only a coincidence. Probably I'd picked up one of those 24-hour flu viruses and it was already gone. I felt relieved, but also a little disappointed. Maybe I really had wanted something extraordinary to happen to me.

And then I went to brush my teeth.

It was only in the bathroom in my pajamas that I noticed the palm of my hand again. I was reaching for the toothpaste when I saw the markings and stood dead still. They weren't purple anymore but more midnight blue, and they were in the shape of a crescent moon and three stars, the exact image – only in reverse – of the markings on the amulet. I tried scrubbing my hands with soap, but the markings didn't come off or even fade a little. They were in my skin, like they'd become part of me.

Coming out of the bathroom, I almost ran into my mother. Quickly I clenched my palm and put it behind my back.

"I just wanted to say good night, honey," she said, kissing me on the forehead. "I'm glad that you've come to accept your father's and my decision about, well, about you-know-what. Sometimes we really do know what's best."

"Oh, sure," I said. "Well, good night." I backed away from her, smiling stiffly and keeping my hand hidden, until I got to my own door and sidled my way into my room. I didn't even try to sleep, but just waited for my parents to go to bed, and then forced myself to watch the clock for another half hour, until midnight. Only then did I get up and make my way silently down the hall to the living room. I pushed aside the curtains and hauled up the window, which made a soft thud. I waited again to make sure that nobody had stirred awake and positioned myself in front of the window: feet planted a little apart, arms straight and back a little, hands turned thirty degrees as I had seen my mother do. Now I tilted up my chin. I remembered what my mother had said to me not long after I had discovered her secret. I think she liked being able to talk about it. "Position is important, Eleanor," she had said, "but it won't get you off the ground. Only your mind can do that. Your mind is the engine. This is the part that can't be taught. You need absolute calm. You need to feel happy and unafraid. You need to think *up*. You have to try not to talk to yourself inside your head. Words don't work. You have to let your mind go beyond language."

Thinking back on what she said, I felt that I knew, sort of, what she meant. Now I resisted the urge to scratch an itch on the side of my nose, and closed my eyes. I tried to relax. I could feel the soft May air on my face. I thought *up*. Then I let the word vanish so that just the feeling was left.

A tingling in my feet.

The breeze picked up and I felt my pajama top fluttering against my stomach. A pleasant humming began in my brain. I felt good and light and the wind definitely picked up some more, but I didn't know what to do next, and finally I opened my eyes to see darkness and the shadowy

35

branches of the tree just in front of me. When I looked down, I saw the night below and the yellow glow of the porch light illuminating the figures of the fountain. Next door I saw the glint of the Worthingtons' basketball hoop and, two streets away, a cat slinking across a garage roof.

I was *flying*.

Immediately my body started to tremble and I dropped down some three feet. *Don't get excited*, I told myself. *Keep calm.* I settled in the air again. *That's it, easy does it.*

I decided to try to move. Concentrating, I lowered my right shoulder and began to glide through the air in an arc. Then the other way, gradually gaining altitude, then lower again. Before I knew it, I was three streets from my house. I went as far as the local community center, with its swimming pool and tennis courts below, and then over the trees of the park. It was the most glorious sensation I had ever felt. I wanted to keep going, but decided not to overdo it the first time and headed back to the house. Before I got there, I began to feel tired and an ache developed in my legs. I was very glad to see my own house again and, thinking that I wouldn't have the accuracy to come down through the window, I decided to land in the backyard instead. My feet touched the grass and my mind let go just as my legs crumpled under me, and I collapsed to the ground.

I rested a moment before climbing through the window back into the house. In bed again, I was so tired that I could hardly even smile as sleep overcame me.

5

VANISHED

At breakfast my father was in a serious funk, walking back and forth across the kitchen floor, stopping to reread the sheet of paper in his hand and shake his head. "I don't understand it. How can a fountain just disappear? Vanish in the night? It doesn't make sense."

"What's that, honey?" my mother said. She was running late, straightening her skirt and brushing her hair even as she came to the table. Usually she was late in the morning after she'd gone on one of her own flying expeditions. Could she have left after I had returned and gone to bed?

"A fountain," Dad said, smacking the paper in his hand. "I got an E-mail today from the mayor of Rome. A small fountain with a marble dolphin spouting water out of its mouth at the corner of two streets. In the morning, it was just gone."

"I'm sure it will turn up. I mean, it can't have just walked away."

"This sounds like a job for Googoo-man," said my brother.

"Please, Solly," Dad said, "not now."

My brother shrugged and kept eating his cereal, the strap of the bathing cap dangling by his chin.

"I don't like it," Dad went on, continuing to pace. "I don't like it at all."

"What's the big deal?" I said. Maybe I was feeling a bit too sure of myself, having flown the night before. "After all, it's just one fountain. They've got lots of them in Rome."

"But each one is different. And special in its own way."

"If you say so, Dad." The truth was, it was hard for me to worry about fountains at this moment. I took a spoonful of my own cereal and then I sneakily looked at my open palm, resting in my lap under the table. The blue moon and stars were still there, although they looked as if they'd maybe faded a little. It suddenly occurred to me to look at my mother's palm; after all, she must have the markings on her hand too. How was it that I had never noticed before? Right now her hand was around her coffee cup and, when she was done, she immediately reached down to grasp the handle of her briefcase, kissed each of us in turn, and headed out the door.

"Milk builds strong muscles, good for fighting the evil

Kaspar Snit," said Solly, picking up his cereal bowl and drinking the remains of the sweetened milk.

"It must be nice to be a kid," my father said, carefully folding the E-mail and slipping it into his shirt pocket. "When you're a kid, you can make everything up. All right, you two. Off to school."

The next night I flew again, and the night after that too. Each time I went a little farther, but not so far that I lost my way or couldn't be back within an hour. It was such an amazing feeling, gliding through the dark sky, knowing the whole world was down there below me. I felt free and light and confident and happy. But on the second night I had a close call with my mother, who was just taking off for her own night flight as I was about to come down for a landing. Fortunately I saw her lifting off through the window, eyes still closed, and I managed to veer sharply to the left to avoid her, landing in the Worthingtons' hydrangea bushes, just like she had once. I was sure she must have heard me, but probably assumed it was the Worthingtons' cat because she didn't come down again. As soon as she was out of sight, I scrambled back into the house through the open window.

In school during the day, I found myself dreaming up conversations:

Guess what, Julia? I can fly.

Hey, Julia, ever see a person rise into the air before? Watch this!

Oooh, Julia, yoo-hoo, look up here. . . .

Oh, the million things that I thought of saying to Julia Worthington while I watched her play her harp on the stage of Inkpotts Public School at the morning music assembly. Of course it's wrong to brag, every kid knows that, but still I wanted badly to show her that there was something really great I could do. Only my desire to show off died after Julia came down from the stage and joined our class again.

"I was good, wasn't I?" Julia said. "Really, I was the best of the whole assembly and I'm sure I got the loudest applause. That fifth grade violin player isn't bad, but he doesn't put much feeling into the music. My dad always says that I have a maturity in my playing that's way beyond my years. You don't think I played the Mozart a little too *legato*, do you? No, I'm sure it was just right. *Whew*, I'm always so tired after a performance. My parents always let me have dinner on the sofa afterward, watching TV, while they bring me anything I want. They say it's very important that I am able to deal with all the stress."

No, I decided, I wouldn't tell Julia. Suddenly I didn't want to use it to make me seem important. Besides, wasn't I really the same Eleanor as before? Sure, I could fly now and it felt great. But it wasn't as if I felt transformed, or something. I wondered why. Maybe it was because it had been too easy, because all I had done was fly around the neighborhood. I would have to think about this.

Since I wouldn't tell Julia about my flying, I wanted at least to tell Solly, which would be better than telling nobody at all. But I didn't know if I could trust him not to run to Mom and Dad and tattle on me. So, walking home with Solly for lunch, I bit my tongue and didn't say anything.

Since my father worked at home, he was the one who gave us lunch and kept us company. But I knew something was wrong today because he just left our lunch on the kitchen table, with a note saying that he had to get back to work. Mom always said that Dad was naturally absent-minded and we shouldn't be too hard on him when he forgot where he parked the car, or when he wore one white running shoe and one brown loafer; but today his thoughts must really have been elsewhere. He had left us sand-wiches, the likes of which I had never seen before – peanut butter with strips of red licorice on whole wheat. Solly was more than happy with our meal. "Googoo-man has a new favorite!" he declared. "This is going to give me extra googoo powers." Then, taking a bite, he found the sand-wich so gooey that it chewed like bubble gum. This made him grin even more.

Solly wanted to knock on Dad's office door on our way back to school to tell him that he ought to try marshmal-low spread with the licorice next time, but I decided that we'd better not disturb him. My father's office wasn't like the office of any other father I had ever met. First of all it was in the garage, which meant that we had to keep our little Fiat car in the driveway all year round. (Nobody else around here drove a Fiat, but it was from Italy, and of course my father was wild about anything from Italy.) And second of all, it was an exact replica of the dormitory in the Fountain of Moses in Rome.

The Fountain of Moses was like a big marble building with three arches and a statue in each. Water flowed from under the statues and also from the mouths of four stone lions. In the back was a private door. It was for the watermen – workers who looked after Rome's fountains and lived *inside* the Fountain of Moses. That was over four hundred years ago but my father's office looked just like this dormitory, with neat beds in a row, a desk to work on, and even a little stove with his espresso coffeemaker on top. On one of the beds lay the mandolin on which he played Italian songs when he was thinking. My father said that the noise of the fountain made him feel calm while he worked, just the way the waters of the Fountain of Moses used to soothe the watermen of Rome.

When Solly and I came home after school, Dad was still in his office. When Mom arrived, she frowned on hearing that Dad had not come out at lunch, but she didn't say anything. She let me do my homework on the kitchen table while she made supper, and then I helped to set out the dishes.

Mom sent Solly to bring Dad in for supper, but all through the meal he hardly said a word. Finally, when Dad let his tartuffo ice cream melt in his bowl did Mom finally say something.

"All right, Manfred. What's going on?"

My father did not look up, but only stirred his ice-cream soup in the bowl. "The Trevi Fountain is gone."

"Gone?"

"That's right. Gone. Vanished. Disappeared."

"But it can't be gone, Manfred. It isn't small like the first one that disappeared. It's enormous. It takes up almost an entire square in Rome."

I knew what my mother was talking about because my father had given me an old etching of the Trevi Fountain, which hung over my bed. It had full-sized human figures and horses and rocks and waterfalls flowing into a great pool around which hundreds of people gathered every day. My father once told me that if you threw a coin into the Trevi Fountain, you would be guaranteed to return to Rome someday.

"I know it doesn't make sense," Dad said. "It weighs thousands of pounds. And why would anyone take it? People travel from all over the world just to see the Trevi Fountain. Remember, Daisy, how you and I threw in our coins on our last day in Rome? And now it isn't there anymore."

After dinner, Dad went to check the computer, only to come back almost immediately. "There's another E-mail from the mayor of Rome. Two more fountains have been stolen. That's the word that the mayor uses here – stolen. There's no other explanation possible. Somebody is stealing the fountains of Rome! He asked me to keep it a secret. They don't want people to panic, or tourists to stop coming to visit. City workers have put up tarpaulins on scaffoldings, with signs saying the fountains are under repair. But how long will they be able to keep that up? And who would do such a thing?"

43

My father had an actual tear in his eye. Maybe only Manfred Blande could cry over a fountain. But it was weird, I felt like crying too, even though I'd never even seen them in real life.

Solly had dipped the end of his napkin in a water glass and was using the wet corner to clean the lenses of his goggles. "The evil Kaspar Snit has struck again," he said. "Stealing beauty from the world."

"I wish you were right," Dad said. "At least we'd know what was going on." And although he usually helped with the dishes, now he got up and walked out of the kitchen. I knew that he was going back to his dormitory office, his watery refuge.

Later, after our fountain was turned off, I could hear through my open bedroom window the sad tremolo of his mandolin.

6

A NATIONAL
EMERGENCY

The blue markings on my hand lasted for about a week.
When they had faded away completely, I couldn't fly
anymore – or so I discovered on trying that same night. I
stood in front of the window, legs apart, hands in position,
chin up, but all that happened was a sort of fluttering in
my feet that kept fading out, as if I were a car that couldn't
quite start. I had to sneak outside, open the fountain's
little secret door, and press the amulet into my palm
again. This time I didn't have any of those flu-like symp-
toms, and the markings were blue from the start, not
green and then purple. Now I knew why I had seen my
mother at the amulet; like me, she had to renew the markings in order to keep on flying.

After that I took off without a hitch, making a nice circuit around the neighborhood, then following the old train tracks for a while before reluctantly heading home again. Now that I had gained confidence, I was getting the urge to fly farther, but I was worried about getting home on time so I held myself back.

"It's missing!" my father said at breakfast, holding another E-mail in his hand. "La Barcaccia! And five others. It's a catastrophe."

I'd never seen my dad look so upset. I knew that La Barcaccia, or the "Leaky Boat," was one of his favorite Roman fountains. Set at the bottom of the Spanish Steps, it was a stone boat sunk into a basin. The small spouts filled it with water, which poured out from all sides. My father had explained that the artist who made it had cleverly taken advantage of the low water pressure at that particular spot, which wasn't strong enough to send the water high. It was a special favorite with kids, Dad had said, and now it was gone.

"They're not going to be able to keep this secret for long," Mom said.

My mother was right. That afternoon the story of the disappearing fountains of Rome was all over the news. Dad went to the magazine shop and bought newspapers from all over the world – *The London Telegraph*, *Le Devoir* from Paris, *The New York Times*, even papers from Moscow, Hong Kong, and Mexico City. All of them showed pictures of piazzas, or squares, with people standing glumly beside the places where the fountains had stood. Now there was just broken stone and torn ends of pipes.

When I came into the living room after finishing my homework, I found Dad and Solly watching the news on television – Dad standing with his arms crossed and Solly munching popcorn like he was enjoying a movie. I looked at the TV, where a news reporter was talking into a microphone. He had a really bad wig on his head – it looked like a hairy baseball glove. I started to listen to what he was saying:

At last count, 153 fountains have disappeared from this great city of Rome. Right behind me stood the Fountain of the Naiads, a real beauty. Yesterday it was here and this morning – poof! – gone. Ten minutes ago, the government of Italy declared a national emergency. The army has been mobilized. Tourists by the thousands are canceling their trips. Meanwhile, the Roman citizens are so upset by the disappearance of their fountains that they are no longer lingering in the public squares. Restaurants are deserted. Right beside me here I have Alberto Agostino, who runs the flower stall behind us. Mr. Agostino, do you speak English?

A little, yes.

Mr. Agostino, how is the flower business these days?
Ah, terrible! Nobody wants.

Mr. Agostino, you're scrunching up your hat there. Tell me, why are the people of Rome so miserable? Things can't be that bad.

But you don't understand, Signor. Without beauty,
life is not worth living.

My father used the remote to turn off the TV.

"Hey," Solly said, "it was just getting good."

"I hadn't heard about the Fountain of the Naiads," Dad said. "The mayor of Rome sent me another E-mail today. He asked if I had any idea who would do such a hateful thing. But I don't."

An idea came to me. "Dad," I said, "maybe you do know. You have all those files in your office of people you've worked for, or who have written to you for information. It could be one of them."

My father looked at me and his eyes widened. He slapped the coffee table with his hand. "You're right, Eleanor! Why didn't I think of that? It could be somebody in my files. Anyway, it's certainly worth a try. I'll go through every last one of them, no matter how long it takes. Thanks for the suggestion . . ." he said, bounding out of the room.

We hardly saw my father for the next three days. He worked day and night, making pots of powerful espresso to keep himself awake. Whenever he did come out of his office and into the house, he would be holding an open file folder and reading the papers inside it. Dark shadows formed under his eyes. On the third night, Mom and I went into the dormitory to bring him a sandwich and a glass of milk since he had not come in for supper. We found him asleep on one of the dormitory beds, a file folder covering his face. Mom gently removed the folder, tucked a blanket up to his chin, and turned out the light.

On these nights I did not go flying. I thought that since my father was up all night, he might come out of his office and see me taking off, or landing, or even gliding overhead. Besides, it just didn't seem right. Each day the number of missing fountains went up and it hardly seemed fair that while this international crisis was going on, and my father desperately trying to find a clue as to who might be the suspect, I should be having the time of my life.

One night, getting ready for bed in my room, I heard a knock on the wall. *Thunk thunk thunka-thunka-thunk*. It was the special Googoo-man knock that Solly had insisted I learn. I went out to the hall and to his door, giving the same knock. The door opened and I saw Solly standing in his underwear.

"What are you doing?" I asked. "You're supposed to be in bed."

"Quick, come inside." He pulled me in, shutting the door behind us. "I need you to time me."

"Huh?"

He handed me the windup cooking timer, in the shape of an egg, from the kitchen. "See, I've been practising," he said. "In case the Googoo-alarm goes off." He pointed up and, looking, I saw that he had hung from his ceiling light a large bell made from an empty tin can, with a metal bolt for the clapper. Solly pulled the string; it sounded like a cowbell more than an alarm. "You see," he said, "I've got my outfit arranged here on the chair. I've got to be able to spring out of bed and become Googoo-man in under three minutes. So I need you to time me."

"All right, but just this once. And then it's bed. One . . . two . . . three. . . ."

"No, wait! I have to get into bed first. Then you have to sound the alarm."

I rolled my eyes. "Well, get into bed then."

He did, pulling up his covers. I checked the timer in my hand and then pulled the string on the tin-can bell. Solly pretended to be waking up; he fluttered open his eyes, sat up, and a look of steely determination came over his face. Then he leapt out of bed and began transforming himself into Googoo-man. First he pulled on his green pajamas. Then he yanked up the bathing suit. Next came the swim flippers. Throwing on the PROPERTY OF HOTEL SCHMUTZ cape and doing up the safety pin was a little trickier. The rubber bathing cap and goggles were a cinch.

I looked at the timer; he was still under two minutes. I didn't want to break his concentration by speaking out loud, but I couldn't help rooting for him in my head. *Come on, Solly, you can do it!* Now came the superelastic belt needed to hold his sonic blaster and neutronic knocker, and which he had left in a neat coil on the seat of the chair. Solly began winding it around his waist by spinning quickly, but it seemed endlessly long and, as he turned and turned, he started to wobble. He was getting dizzy! The elastic began to slip downward, so that it was winding not around his waist but his hips, and then his legs, and finally his ankles.

"Be careful, Sol –"

Too late. He lost his balance and teetered over. Fortunately there was a pillow on the floor by the chair, just where his face landed with an *oomph!* He lay there, face-down, the elastic tight around his legs. There is nothing more pathetic than a superhero lying on his face, tied up with elastic.

"You okay?" I asked, looking down at him.

"Fine" came the muffled reply. "What's my time?"

I looked at the timer. "Two minutes and forty-three seconds."

"Pretty good," he said.

"Yeah. It's just too bad you can't move."

For a moment he didn't say anything.

"I think I need more practice."

7

THE LAST
FOUNTAIN

Coming home from school with Solly, I noticed that the door leading into my father's office was open. I sent Solly into the house and then went over to the door and stepped inside. And gasped. Dad had always kept the place immaculate and precisely ordered – the beds perfectly made, papers neatly arranged on the desk, pencils and pens in their little glass stand. But now it looked as if a tornado had touched down in the room, sending files and papers, cups and plates, blankets and pillows whirling about and landing every which way. All the file-cabinet drawers were open and the contents strewn everywhere. Even my father's pretty, round-backed mandolin lay on the floor.

Was it the work of vandals? It took me a moment to realize that my father himself had made the mess, taking my suggestion to heart and tearing apart his dormitory office in search of clues to the identity of the fountain thief. He wasn't in the office now so I headed into the house, where I found my dad, my mom, and Solly in the kitchen.

"Did you find any clues, Dad?" I asked.

"Not one, Eleanor," he said, with disappointment. "Not one suspect even. And look at this –"

He held up the newspaper. On the front page were two headlines in giant black letters:

LAST FOUNTAIN IN ROME DISAPPEARS
COUNTRY PREPARES FOR WAR

"The very last fountain gone," my father said. "It was a small wall fountain called the Porter. It was a carving of a man holding a small barrel, with a gentle stream of water pouring from it. Everybody in Rome loved that little fountain. Now what's left? Just some broken bricks. And look at this," Dad said, pointing to the newspaper. "The government is calling it the work of enemy countries. They're preparing to go to war."

"That's just terrible," Mom said. "But war with whom?"

"With anybody. With everybody! This is going to be a disaster of world proportions."

For a moment none of us said a word. Then the silence was broken by a soft *aherk!* Solly had taken his bicycle horn from under his elastic belt and gently squeezed the rubber bulb.

"I wish I had a bigger sonic blaster," he said.

It was a dream that woke me up. A dream that I was flying over the school and that all the other kids were standing on the roof, including Julia Worthington with her harp, and that they had turned away from Julia to stare up at me in awe.

I was hungering to really fly, not just dream about it, as a way to forget about everything that was going on, but it didn't seem like a good idea. Still, there was no harm in just getting up, so I pushed off the covers and stood in my dark bedroom. No sounds came from anywhere; there was just the curtains blowing a little more than usual at my window. I tiptoed down the hall, peering every which way, but there was nothing. I could always go into the kitchen and find something to eat. Wasn't there a leftover piece of chocolate cake in the refrigerator? But I wasn't very hungry. So I went into the living room instead.

The windows were closed. *It's always nice to get a little fresh air*, I thought, unlatching a window and hauling it up. It went *thump* and I held my breath, waiting to see if anyone stirred. Again, nothing. The wind felt good on my face. It blew my pajamas against my body. What would be the harm in a short flight around the block?

I opened my palm and held it close to my face so that I could see the moon and the three stars. They were a little faded, but not so much that I needed to worry about getting a new imprint from the amulet. I got in position: legs apart, arms back, chin up, eyes closed. *Relax*, I told myself, *just relax*. Maybe it was sheer anticipation that made me so buoyant, but before I knew it I was opening my eyes to the night sky. The air was cooler than it had been the last few days and I had to admit that the wind was a little more forceful than I was used to, but I was sure it was nothing that I couldn't handle.

I got some more altitude and then did a wide bank, circling to the north and following a little creek that ran through the valley between the subdivisions. A raindrop touched my cheek. The tailwind gave me more speed than I'd ever had before, and I zipped along so quickly that it felt as exciting as a rollercoaster ride. For a long time I hardly even noticed what passed beneath me, until I looked just ahead and saw the Ferris wheel of Conlin's Amusement Park, shut down for the night but still winking its blue and yellow lights.

Conlin's was more than a hundred miles from my house. I could hardly believe I'd gotten so far and hurriedly I turned around, veering too close to the ground so that I had to climb again. How tiring it was to gain height, and even when I leveled off the flying did not become much easier. Now the wind was hurling itself at me so that it felt like swimming against a strong current – more so because the rain really began to slant down. Drops stung my cheeks and made me wince. It was difficult to keep on course and stay in the right frame of mind. I would suddenly become frightened and my body would shudder and plunge until I could focus and steady myself again.

It seemed like forever before I began to see the familiar landmarks that showed I was approaching home. How thankful I was to see the round water tower, the hockey arena, even the red striped roof of Rooster's Fried Chicken. I tried to cheer myself up by remembering the time that Solly insisted that a rooster wouldn't ever eat a chicken. That, he said, would be "cannonball-ism." I couldn't wait to get out of my cold, soaking clothes and into my bed, where I would be warm and safe. I didn't even care about having to explain to my mother in the morning just why my clothes *were* soaking wet.

I was ten streets away, then seven, then five, when I knew that something was wrong.

At first I couldn't tell what, except that, as I approached my street, it seemed darker than the others around. Also, there was an ominous thrumming sound, a kind of mechanical drone coming from somewhere ahead. I came up over the last row of houses before our own and the drone became a great roaring noise. Large black forms, about as high as I was, blocked my view, with the air above them a gleaming whir. It took me a long moment to realize that they were helicopters – four black hulking helicopters – rotary blades turning as they hovered over our house.

What were they doing there? An awful sound arose, a screeching and groaning, like something was being wrenched apart. The helicopters began to shake violently and then suddenly rise. As the helicopters continued to go up, I could see what had caused the awful noise. Each one had an iron chain attached, leading downwards to our fountain, which they were hauling into the air.

They were stealing *our* fountain!

How could they do that? I was so mad that it took me a moment to realize something else. Along with the fountain they were stealing the amulet, hidden in the secret compartment!

The helicopters strained with the load as the fountain swayed beneath. They turned towards the east, continuing to beat upwards with their long blades. These had to be the same thieves who had stolen the fountains of Rome. I rose to follow them, but I must have got too close because the tremendous force of the draft from the helicopter blades hit me full-on. I tumbled backwards, somersaulting through the air.

Head over heels I went, over and over through the night sky. I heard a voice screaming – my own. I forced out my hands and feet, slowing down and gaining just enough control so as not to shatter all my bones as I hit the grass of the Worthingtons' front yard. The next thing I knew, I was flat on my back – limbs splayed out, the back of my head throbbing from its knock on the ground. It was a good thing that Mr. Worthington had the best grass on the street, like a plush carpet.

For a long moment I just lay there, stunned. Our front door flew open and I raised myself enough to see my father dash out in his pajamas, followed by my mother. "Our fountain!" he cried. "They've stolen our fountain! This is too much! It's wicked! Dastardly! Inhuman! Unbearable! It's the end of everything!"

He stood amid the rubble of our front yard and put his hands over his face. My mother went up and hugged him. Solly came through the front door, almost tripping on his flippers as he adjusted his goggles.

"That darn superelastic belt," Solly said. "I should have been out here sooner. Don't worry, Daddy. Googoo-man will bring our fountain back."

He pulled his sonic blaster from his belt and held it in the air. "Cover your ears!" he shouted, and then gave the rubber end two big squeezes. *Aherk! Aherk!* When the helicopters didn't come back, he turned the horn around and peered into it, as if something might be broken.

Mom spotted me and hurried over. "Are you all right?" she whispered, helping me up. Her voice sounded both scared and angry. "You could have been killed."

"Mom, I saw them! There were four helicopters. And they headed east. I was . . . I was flying," I admitted.

"I thought maybe you were," she said, with a sigh. Keeping her hands on my shoulders, she steered me towards our house. "All right, everyone. Back inside."

8

THE EMPTY
SPACE

Inside the house, it was chaos. Dad was bewailing the theft of our fountain, pulling on his own hair like he was going to yank himself right off the ground. Solly kept shaking and squeezing his sonic blaster, as if to figure out why it had failed to bring down four giant helicopters. Mom was trying to calm down Dad and get Solly to stop honking the bicycle horn, all the while filling a bag with ice to put it on the sore bump on the back of my head.

And then things got *worse*. The phone started ringing; sirens screamed as police cars and fire trucks converged on our house. Television reporters with cameras, microphones, and powerful electric lights began pouring out of their vans, blocking the road. How they had all found out so quickly we didn't know, but here they were.

The firefighters clomped around our house with their boots, pickaxes and extinguishers in their hands. The policemen and policewomen stood around with notepads, trying to make sense of things. The reporters videotaped the space where the fountain used to be and interviewed the neighbors, who had come out see what all the commotion was about. Solly turned on the television and there was our neighbor Mr. Worthington in a bathrobe, with a hair net on his head, standing in front of our house with the words *Coming to you live!* flashing on the bottom of the screen. While Mr. Worthington talked seriously about "the reputation of this fine neighborhood" into the reporter's microphone, Julia and Jeremy beside him made faces at the camera. So that was how the reporters had found out – Mr. Worthington had phoned them.

"Nincompoops," Solly said, turning off the television.

At last the firefighters, police officers, and reporters got into their cars and trucks and vans and drove away, while the neighbors went back to their houses. The four of us sat in the living room for a long while without talking. Finally my mother said, "Okay, everybody, time to get some sleep. That means you too, Manfred. We all need to get our energy back. The Blande family is not defeated, not by a long shot. Right?"

Nobody said anything.

I said, "Right, Googoo-man?"

Solly pulled the goggles from his face. He took off his rubber cap, his cape, and his swim flippers. "How can a kid be a superhero, anyway?" he said. Then he wrapped everything up in the cape, went to his room, and put himself to bed.

Of course the theft of our fountain wasn't as important as those in Rome, but my father took it just as hard. He spent the entire next day, from morning until evening, just standing on the sidewalk and staring at the space where the fountain used to be. On our way to school, Solly and I stood beside him for a few minutes. This was the first time I could remember Solly not going to school in his Googooman outfit. Instead, he wore a T-shirt with a Tyrannosaurus rex on it, a pair of brown pants with a stretchy waist, and sneakers. His hair was neatly parted and combed to one side. He looked, well, like just a regular kid. For months and months that was just what I had wanted – a brother who didn't go around in fancied-up pajamas thinking he was a caped crusader. And now that I had one he seemed just . . . just ordinary.

Solly and I stood beside my father, looking at the broken stone and the torn end of pipe. Solly said, "It was a really great fountain, Dad."

"Thanks, son," Dad said.

There was nothing else to do but go to school.

A strange thing happened at school. As we entered the yard, the kids stopped playing. Skipping ropes slowed down until they lay on the ground. Tennis balls bounced off the wall and didn't get thrown back. The kids all stared at Solly and me, then turned their eyes down like they didn't know what to say. Solly reached out to take my hand and that was how we walked into the school.

At his classroom door, Solly said, "Meet me here when school's out, okay?"

"Okay, Solly."

In class, I found it hard to concentrate. Mr. Bentham was sitting on his favorite perch atop the filing cabinet, his scalp almost grazing the ceiling, eyes closed. First we did math, then social science, and then we had a silent reading period, during which Mr. Bentham appeared to go to sleep. Everyone in class kept glancing up at him, sure that he was going to topple off the cabinet.

Mr. Bentham opened his eyes. "All right, class, silent reading is over. Please put away your books. I want to say a few words. We are very fortunate to live in such a peaceful country and to have so many advantages. But sometimes the ugly events of the world intrude even here, reminding us that we are indeed a part of a greater society. One of those events has happened to our fellow classmate, Miss Blande. I'm sure we all wish to offer our condolences to Miss Blande and her family for the loss of their fountain. It was a landmark in our neighborhood, one of the things that made this place both unique and special. We can only hope that your fountain will be found again, Miss Blande, but we want you to know that our thoughts are with you. Right, class?"

The whole class nodded its assent. "Yes, yes," and "That's right," and "We're with you, Eleanor" came from all around me. I didn't know what to say, but only blushed and lowered my eyes. At that moment I thought that Mr. Bentham must be the greatest teacher on the entire planet.

As I promised, I met Solly at his classroom door and the two of us walked home together. I thought of how the fountain had embarrassed me and how often I had wished for it to disappear, just the way I had wanted Solly to dress like a normal kid. And now here was Solly holding my hand, which he would never have done before today, and here were the two of us going home to our fountainless life and all I could feel was how much I missed the way things had been before.

We got to our street and Solly and I walked along the sidewalk. "It doesn't look right, does it?" Solly said. I knew he was talking about the house. From here we would have already been able to see two of the horses and their riders and we would have heard the constant splash of the water.

"No, it doesn't look right," I said.

To my surprise, it turned out that I wasn't the only person to discover an unexpected affection for our fountain now that it was gone. The empty front yard was filled with flowers – bouquets of roses and lilies, pots of flowering begonias and daffodils. They were beautiful and their scent filled the air. And there was my father, standing on the sidewalk just as he had been when we'd left in the morning.

"Wow, Dad," Solly said. "Where did all the flowers come from?"

"People brought them by. All the neighbors. Your school principal. Mom's co-workers. Even strangers."

"Dad," I said, "aren't you tired, standing there?"

"Not really. Mom's in the house. She came home early."

Solly stayed outside with Dad. Inside, my mother was preparing dinner. "We're going to have a special dinner tonight," she said. "Your father's favorite ravioli. I'm hoping it will cheer him up. I guess it's time you and I had a little talk, Eleanor."

"I guess so," I said, hanging my head. I prepared myself for a lecture – how I wasn't supposed to learn to fly, how it was wrong of me to have spied on my mother and found out about the amulet. I wasn't sure if I should just agree and apologize, or stubbornly defend myself. I guess I felt like doing both.

"Right now," Mom said, "I'm more worried about what might have happened to you when those helicopters came and stole our fountain. We're lucky you didn't get hurt in that fall. My own mother once got shot at by a hunter who thought she was the world's biggest duck, and my grand-mother Esther had to get stitches in her forehead back in the 1920s when she crashed into a weather vane on top of a barn."

"You mean people have been flying in our family since way back then?"

"Even before. Your great-great-grandmother made an expedition to the Middle East in 1901 to visit archeologi-cal sites. I don't know if she found it in some old tomb or bought it in the marketplace, but she brought the amulet home with her. I guess it has caused the women in our family problems ever since. Somebody saw your great-

great-grandmother fly, and accused her of being a witch. She had to convince them that the man had been dreaming."

"Mom," I said softly. "Flying is *so* much fun."

"Isn't it?" She couldn't resist smiling as she bent down and gave me a hug. At that moment, I felt as if Mom and I shared something that was just between us. "I'm still angry at you but I can't help – oh well, you're a Galinski woman for sure," she said. "But now that the amulet is gone, there won't be any flying for either of us. Maybe I should be glad, but I'm not. The truth is, it feels just awful. I'm going to miss flying more than I can say."

How sad my mother looked as she talked of losing the amulet – as sad as Dad looked over the fountains. I turned my hand over and looked at my palm. The moon and three stars were still there, but a little fainter than the day before. Mom saw me and held out her hand too, and for the first time I saw the markings on her palm. They were a little darker, but not much. In about a week, neither of us would be able to fly.

I said, "Maybe whoever stole the fountain doesn't even know the amulet is there."

"Yes, but it could be dangerous if they find it. I remember my mother telling me that if its power doesn't come out one way, it might come out another. And whoever stole the fountain certainly has no good intentions. When my mother gave the amulet to me, she said it would be my responsibility to keep it safe, and I promised her I would. I didn't want to keep it in the house in case you or Solly found it, so I had your father make that little compartment in the fountain. I thought it would be safe there. It never occurred to me that somebody might steal the whole thing."

"We can't let some bad guy have it. And besides, I just learned to fly – I haven't even gone very far yet. We're just going to have to get it back, Mom. And the fountain too."

"I wish we knew how. I wish we knew who was behind it. In the meantime, we've got your father to worry about. He's been standing out there for hours."

I said, "Maybe I should bring him one of the folding lawn chairs. So he can sit down."

"Good idea, Eleanor."

So I did. My father thanked me, then unfolded the chair and sat on the sidewalk in the exact same spot where he had been standing. He didn't seem to want to talk, so I just stood beside him for a while. I saw the door of the next house open and Mr. Worthington step outside. As always, he wore a dark suit and his round bowler hat. After him came Jeremy and Julia. Mr. Worthington closed his front door and came down the steps – he had an odd way of turning sideways as he did so – then along the path to the sidewalk, his children following.

Mr. Worthington approached us and removed his hat. I think that if Jeremy and Julia had been wearing hats, they would have removed them too. Mr. Worthington fiddled with the brim a moment and then noisily cleared his throat.

"Mr. Blande," he said, "as you know I have not been a . . . a friend of your fountain. I have made my opposition to its placement, on our otherwise unblemished street, known to the public at large. Well, I was wrong. Without your fountain, our street is just a street like any other – nothing interesting about it. I would like you to know that I am in the process of circulating a new petition demanding that your fountain be returned immediately by the person or persons responsible."

My father didn't say anything; didn't even get up out of his chair.

Julia Worthington sidled up to me and said, "It's really rotten, Eleanor. Me and Jeremy both think so."

All of us stared at the space where the fountain used to be. The flowers were nice, I thought, but they weren't a replacement. At last my father said, "That is very kind of you, Mr. Worthington. Not that it will do any good, but it is very kind."

"Yes, well," Mr. Worthington muttered, and then, placing his hat back on his head, he turned and walked to his own front door, the junior Worthingtons behind him.

On the way back into the house, I noticed that my father had left his office door open again. I went to close it and saw, once more, the mess inside: papers everywhere, chairs and wastepaper baskets upturned, beds pulled apart. It didn't seem right just to leave it like that, so I went in and made the beds, folding hospital corners like my dad had taught me. I put the mandolin on its little wooden stand and the espresso pot on the stove.

The place looked a little better, but the real disaster was the files everywhere. I didn't know how to put them in proper order in the file cabinets, but at least I could gather up the papers, put them in their file folders, and put the folders in neat piles. That would mean less work for my father when his spirits picked up enough to get back to work. Of course there was no telling whether he'd have any work at all, with all the fountains disappearing.

It wasn't an easy job, figuring out which papers belonged in which files, but I moved along the floor on my knees, doing the best I could. My father had sure worked for a lot of clients over the years. He had helped to build or restore hundreds of fountains that gave pleasure to the people who admired their sculptures, or enjoyed their cooling mists on hot days. It took me an hour to clean up the floor, with only a few files left on one of the beds.

I began picking them up, among them a file folder so thin that it felt empty. But no, there were three pieces of paper still inside. I looked at the name printed in black ink on the folder: RAPSAK T. INS. That was a pretty weird name, but then there had been a lot of foreign sounding names on the files. Still, something about it made me stare at it for a long moment. Then I looked at the sheets inside. The first was a letter from Rapsak T. Ins. The second was a photocopy of my father's reply. The third was another letter from Mr. Ins. As I read them, my heart started pounding. I looked for Rapsak T. Ins' return address, but it wasn't on his letters. And then I found it under the letters, on an envelope. Could this really be true?

"DAD!" I screamed, tripping as I rushed to the door. "Mom! Dad! Solly! I know who the thief is! I know who he is!"

9

THE RAPSAK
LETTERS

I ran out of the dormitory, only to find that the folding lawn chair on the sidewalk was empty. The file folder under my arm, I looked up and down the street as if my father himself had vanished.

The front door opened. "Hey, Eleanor," said Solly. "We were all looking for you. Dinner's ready."

With relief I sprinted up the stairs and followed Solly into the house. Mom must have sent him to take an early bath because his hair was still wet and he was already wearing pajamas with cowboys all over them, the ones that Aunt May had sent for his birthday last year but that he would never wear because he said they were "unsuitable" for a superhero. I guessed they were suitable enough for an ordinary kid.

In the dining room, my mother had put a red and white checked cloth on the table, with candles flickering in the middle and an Italian opera playing on the stereo. Dad was already in his place, and Solly and I sat down while Mom brought in a big bowl of steaming pasta. I had so much to tell them, but suddenly I couldn't find the words.

"This is very nice of you, Daisy," my father said, although, if anything, he looked more downhearted than before. "But it only reminds me of Rome. My beloved Rome is not the same anymore. Just think, Daisy, all the fountains we looked at together are gone. Ripped out! It defies any rational explanation. Remember how we talked last month about taking the kids on a trip to see them?" He looked at the pasta my mother had served onto his plate, a favorite from the time in Italy. "Your meal looks delicious, but I just don't have an appetite."

"It's not going to do anyone any good if you just waste away, Manfred," my mother said. "Please eat. You need your strength."

He pushed the plate away. "I can't. Everyone enjoy yourselves. I think I'll go back outside."

Now I *had* to speak. "Dad, wait," I said. "I *know*."

"Know what, Eleanor?" Mom said.

"I know who stole the fountains."

My father smiled wanly at me. "Eleanor, it warms my heart to see how concerned you are. But of course you don't know. You can't know. Not even the Italian police know."

How exasperating adults can be sometimes! I had no

choice but to shout at the top of my lungs. "I DO SO KNOW! SOLLY WAS RIGHT ALL ALONG!"

Both my parents turned to stare at me. Mom said quietly, "All right, Eleanor. You'd better tell us exactly what you're talking about."

"That's what I'm trying to do. Look at this file I found in Dad's office." I took it from under the chair and put it on the table.

My father craned his neck so that he could read the name. "RAPSAK T. INS," he read aloud. "I remember him vaguely. But he wasn't a client, just someone who wrote to me."

"Yes, Dad, but look what he wrote." I took the first letter out of the file and put it on the table. My mother leaned over to read it to all of us:

From the Desk of Rapsak T. Ins

Dear Mr. Blande,

I am writing to you in regard to your capacity as the foremost expert on fountains in the world. As a retired and reclusive millionaire, I wish to make my private estate the most beautiful spot on Earth. I agree with your belief (stated in your classic book, Fountain Fundamentals) *that fountains are the height of artistic and social achievement.*

My question to you is, how can I build fountains on my property that will not only rival, but actually exceed, the beauty of the fountains of Rome? I will pay you handsomely to act as my chief consultant.

I expect a reply from you posthaste.

Yours,

Rapsak T. Ins, Millionaire

"*Mmm,*" my father ruminated. "That is an odd letter, I admit. I'd half forgotten about it, probably because it seemed so ridiculous. But still, I don't quite see what you're getting at, Eleanor."

"Here's your answer to him, Dad," I said, pulling the second sheet from the file. This time it was my father who, peering through his reading glasses, read aloud:

Dear Mr. Ins,

While I appreciate your recognition of the value of fountains, I fear that I cannot help you. It would be impossible to exceed, or even match, the beauty of the fountains of Rome. They were built by the greatest sculptors and designers, over a period of centuries, and for a setting – Rome – that is a jewel in itself. Even attempting such a feat would be hubris of the worst kind.

Yours sincerely,

Manfred Blande

Solly said, "What does 'hubris' mean, Daddy?"

"It's an ancient Greek word that comes from mere humans trying to outdo the gods. It means arrogance and folly. Rapsak T. Ins is a foolish man to think that he can simply buy beauty. I knew that I would never be able to satisfy him, and so I turned down the job. And that was the end of that."

"But it wasn't, Dad," I said. I pulled the last sheet of paper from the file. "Look. He wrote back one more time. I'll read this one."

From the Desk of Rapsak T. Ins

Dear Mr. Blande,

Hubris? How dare you! You do not have any idea who you are insulting. I shall prove you wrong. If I cannot make my estate more beautiful than Rome, then I shall have Rome in my own backyard.

Yours,

Rapsak T. Ins, Millionaire

"Let me see that," Dad said, frowning. "I suppose I just put it out of my mind. How absurd. The man turned out to be even more pompous than I thought. But, Eleanor, people write things they don't mean or can't really do. Why do you think he has anything to do with the thefts? It could just be a coincidence."

"Our fountain got stolen too, Manfred," Mom said. "So whoever did it must also have a grudge against you. Like this man."

"Mom's right," I said. "And look at the name! Look carefully."

We all stared at the name on the file. Even Solly, who was still learning to read. In fact, it was Solly who began to spell out the name, but because of his dyslexia, he started at the wrong end and began to spell it out backwards.

"S . . . N . . . I . . . T," he said slowly. "K . . . A . . . S . . . P . . . A . . . R."

"Snit!" my father cried in amazement. "Kaspar Snit!"

My mother's eyes widened. "But how can that be? There isn't such a person. I mean, there can't be. Solly made him up. Kaspar Snit is just the bad guy that Googoo-man has to fight. You did make him up, didn't you, Solly?"

We all turned to look at my little brother. He cast his eyes down as if he had been caught doing something wrong.

"Tell us, Solly, tell us!" My father's voice rose almost to a shout. "Who *is* Kaspar Snit?"

At that moment poor Solly did the only thing he could. He burst into tears. It was a sorry sight, seeing a former superhero crying until his nose began to drip.

"Solly, Solly," cooed my mother, putting her arms around him. "It's okay, honey, nobody's angry at you."

My father crouched down to kiss him. "I'm sorry if I upset you, Solly-Polly. I just got excited, that's all. You told us right at the start and we didn't take you seriously. That's our fault."

Solly's sniffles slowed down. "Now you just take your time," Mom said, stroking his hair. "We need to know about this Kaspar Snit. What is it that you always call him?"

"The evil genius," Solly said. "Because he is – he's the most evil genius in the world."

"And where is it you always say he lives?"

I answered this one. "In a fortress in the Verulian Mountains."

"That's right," Solly said. "Dad, where are the Verulian Mountains anyway?"

"Very far from here, across the ocean and all the way to eastern Europe. On the other side of the Carpathian mountain range. It's the last uninhabited region of Europe."

"I meant to show you before," I said. "Look at the return address on Rapsak T. Ins' envelope."

I took it out of the file and turned it over. And there was the address, engraved in blood red ink:

Rapsak T. Ins
Mount Darkling
Verulia 023210

"This just gets weirder and weirder," my mother said. She turned back to my brother. "Now, Solly, this is very, very important. How do you know about Kaspar Snit?"

"It's on the tape."

"What tape?"

"One of the story tapes in my room. I listen to it on my tape recorder all the time."

My parents looked at each other. "Show us," Dad said.

Solly paused a moment and then raced towards his bedroom, the rest of us following him. I came after Solly while my parents practically elbowed each other in the doorway to get into the room. My brother slid under his bed to dig out his tape recorder; he liked to listen to it under there, as if he were in a cave. It was one of those brightly colored recorders, with big buttons made for kids. All this time I thought he'd been under there listening to "The House at Pooh Corner" and "The Mouse and the Motorcycle." He plucked a tape from the pile on his dresser and held it up triumphantly.

"Here it is. I've had it for such a long time. At least since I was six."

"That's over a year ago," said Dad. "Not long after I got those letters."

"I remember," I said. "You got a story tape in the mail, Solly, without any return address on it. Mom thought it must have come from Aunt May."

"Yup."

"And you listened to the tape, then?" Dad asked.

"About a trizillion times. I know it off by heart."

He started to speak in a deep, vibrating voice. It reminded me of Dracula in an old movie I once saw. "*My name is Kaspar Snit,*" Solly intoned. "*I am not a nightmare. Not a story. I am a real person. . . .*" He grinned. "You see?"

Mom said, "I think it was around that time that you started to become Googoo-man."

This time Solly didn't answer.

"Were you scared, Solly? Is that why you became Googoo-man?"

Again he didn't answer, but just looked up at us with his big eyes.

"You're a very bright boy," Dad said, giving Solly a hug. "Now I think you'd better play that tape for us."

"Sure," Solly said. He smacked a button on the recorder with his fist, popped in the tape, slammed it closed, and hit the PLAY button.

10

THE VOICE
ON THE TAPE

[Sound of ominous music.] The voice on the tape begins:

My name is Kaspar Snit. I am not a nightmare. [Thunderclap.] *Not a story. I am a real person. My home is a fortress, high in the Verulian Mountains.* [Sound of violent windstorm.] *An immense wall surrounds me, with a guard tower rising at each corner. My warrior army obeys my every command.* [Footsteps of a thousand marching soldiers.] *I am the most powerful individual on Earth, as powerful as many countries!*
[Music swells.]
Is anyone more mean than I am?
[Chorus of voices]: *No!*

Is anyone a bigger spoilsport?

[Chorus of voices]: *No!*

That's right, because I am the one, the only, the EVIL KASPAR SNIT!

[Music grows louder and faster.]

And what is my purpose, you ask?

[Voice of young, sweet child]: *O Mister Snit, what is your purpose?*

To steal the beauty from the world! And why, you might ask, do I wish to steal the beauty from the world?

[Voice of another young, sweet child]: *O Mister Snit, why do you wish to steal the beauty from the world?*

Because I can! Because I want to! Because I don't like you! And, most of all, because of a family. That's right, one little family. The Blandes.

("The Blandes!" cried my father.

"*Shhh*," whispered the rest of us.)

That's right. Manfred. Daisy. Solly. And last but not least, Eleanor Blande.

("Me?" I said with a gulp.

"*Shhh*," whispered the rest of them.)

[Music swells to a deafening crescendo and then descends to the sound of sentimental violins.]

But I was not always this way. No, I was not always the evil Kaspar Snit. Yes, it has taken me a long time and considerable effort to get to the pinnacle upon which I stand today. Once upon a time, I was merely an unpleasant little boy living in a tiny house in Finchley, in the outskirts of London. A little tall for my age perhaps, a little skinny, but otherwise a run-of-the-mill child. My parents loved me as parents should. My teachers were helpful to me. But was this enough for young Kaspar?

[Sound of a boy having a tantrum, kicking feet and pounding hands on ground.]

No, it certainly wasn't enough! I was ambitious. I wanted more. I wanted extra attention. The biggest piece of cake at the birthday party. The most toys. The highest praise. Sharing? Yuck! Playing nice? Fooey! Cooperating? Blah! That was for wimps. I wanted EVERYTHING for myself. And NOTHING for anyone else. I wanted to be prince. King. Emperor. DICTATOR!

[Sound of toy trumpets and drums.]

[Children shouting in unison]: *Hail, Kaspar! Hail, Kaspar!*

All right, so it didn't happen so fast. As soon as I was old enough, I left my parents behind and struck out into the world. I tried a few regular jobs, but they required too much work, not to mention having to be nice to people. I found that less reputable professions suited me better. I started as a petty thief — watches, purses, scarves, anything I could get my hands on. I graduated to fraud, embezzlement, counterfeiting, trafficking in elephant tusks, dumping garbage into the world's oceans . . .

[Sound of falling coins.]

. . . and soon I was rich. Of course it was very pleasant to be rich and to take advantage of unsuspecting people. But was that enough? No, it was not. I had wealth but no power or fame, and I craved both of them like a starving man craves food. But what to do? Well, I did what countless restless and discontented souls

have done before me. I decided to travel. To see something of the world and find the right opportunity for myself.

 And so I visited the great cities of the world – New York, Paris, Madrid, Moscow, Hong Kong, Bombay.
[Voices in different languages, cars honking, bicycle bells ringing.]
Nowhere did I find what I was looking for. And then one day I arrived in Rome.

 ("Rome!" cried my mother.

 "*Shhh!*" whispered the rest of us.)

At first Rome was no different from the other cities. And then one day, walking down the street, I heard something. A voice coming through an open door. Out of curiosity, I went in and saw students sitting in a sort of theater while they listened to a man lecture on the history of Roman fountains. I could not imagine why anyone would listen to such a tedious subject. Out of curiosity, I decided to sit down beside a young man. When the lecture was over, the young man introduced himself. His name was Manfred Blande.

 ("That's you, Daddy," said Solly.

 "*Shhh,*" whispered the rest of us.)

When I told this Manfred Blande that I was a poor traveler named Kaspar "Brown," he immediately invited me to dine with him and his family. Ah, I thought to myself, how amusing it will be to see how regular people live. And so he took me to the attic apartment that required me, being so tall, to stoop when I wasn't sitting down. No doubt I appeared an odd figure to them; by that time I had begun to wear a black cape and pointed beard. But they treated me in the warmest manner possible. Together the husband and wife prepared a modest yet satisfying meal, and they insisted on giving me the largest portion of every dish.

Even their children, a little girl and a baby boy, were friendly to me. The baby, a hideous diapered blob named Solly who could say nothing but "goo-goo," fastened himself to my leg and wouldn't let go. But the worst, the very worst, was the girl. Eleanor.

[Hissing voices]: *Eleanor!*

What that miserable child did not put me through! First, she decided that it was very funny to yank on my beard. Then she made me sing "Mary Had a Little Lamb" – seventeen times! After that it was "Ring Around the Rosie." Imagine, me, Kaspar Snit, who aspired to the greatest evil deeds of all time, singing nursery rhymes! It was a nightmare. And then, after dinner, this girl child, this little walking, talking bundle of revolting enthusiasm, had the nerve to ask me to give her a horsey ride. That's right, a horsey ride. I had to get down on my knees – how utterly humiliating – while she rode on top of me. "Giddy-up, Uncle Kaspy!" she cried, slapping me with a rolled-up newspaper!

[Music swells to a crescendo of cymbal crashes.]

Never have I been so humiliated. I am nobody's uncle and nobody's friend. I am the evil Kaspar Snit! How dare Eleanor Blande and the rest of her obnoxious family treat me as if I were a regular person! But the most insulting moment, the coup de grace, *occurred just as I was leaving. Ah, even now, I can hardly bear to repeat it.*

[Sniveling voices]: *Please tell us, O evil one!*
All right. Manfred Blande shook my hand with disgusting warmth. Daisy thrust a package of leftovers under my arm. I forced myself to pat baby Solly on the head. At last, I thought, I can get away from this family. That was when Eleanor Blande squeezed between her parents, looked up at me with that hideously sweet face, and said:

[Voice of young Eleanor]: *You're nice, Uncle Kaspy.*

Nice? (Crash!) Nice! (Boom!) Kaspar Snit, most evil of all men, NICE! I left that apartment fuming and cursing. The first chance I got, I tossed that package into the gutter and vowed that I would have my vengeance on the Blandes. I would show them who was nice! Yes, I would have my vengeance and with it would begin my reign of evildoing. But not right away. No, first, I had to build my empire.

The very next day I went in search of a land – isolated and forbidding – where I might build my fortress and raise my army. It has taken years, but I have watched with grim satisfaction as the walls of stone have risen. Now, at last, the final stone has been mortared in its place.

I am almost ready. Ready to earn my great power and fame, to make the whole world know and fear me. I shall do so by taking away what others love. I cannot bear the thought of other people – people like the Blandes – kind, decent, weak people living their happy little lives. So I shall begin with a little revenge. I shall steal beauty from the world – what Manfred Blande cherishes the most. It is a devilishly original way to use my power, do you not think? And through the father I will get to that miserable child Eleanor. She and her family will be the first to recognize me for the evil genius that I am. Eleanor Blande will learn that Kaspar Snit is the very opposite of . . . of nice!

Yes, I shall take away from the world what it loves best. And once I begin, no one will be able to stop me. Ha-ha-ha-ha-ha-ha-ha-ha-ha. . . .

11

THE TRUTH
SINKS IN

The tape ran out and the recorder clicked to a stop. For a long moment, nobody said a word. I looked at my parents' faces; they seemed stunned, like someone had just banged them both on the head with a mallet.

My father started to shake his head in disbelief. "Do you remember him, Daisy? That odd fellow I brought home to supper? I haven't thought about him in years."

"But he's been thinking about us," my mother said. "I would never have remembered his name. I thought he was creepy, but also sad. I felt sorry for him. But there was something in the way he looked at us with those hooded eyes, like an eagle about to devour its prey, that made me squirm."

"He had awful table manners," Dad said. "He didn't know how to hold a knife and fork, and he wiped his fingers on his cape. And all this time, while we've been going on with our lives, he's been brooding about that one night!"

"He's been brooding about me!" I said. "I don't remember him at all. Did I really call him Uncle Kaspy?"

My parents looked at each other. "It sounds vaguely familiar," Dad said.

"I think you did," Mom admitted.

"Oh, great," I said with a moan. "And a horsey ride too."

"Yeah, you really, really ticked him off," Solly said. "You aren't supposed to call a guy who wants to be the most evil person in the world *nice*. Big mistake, I'd say."

"Thanks a lot, Solly. So now he's stolen all of the fountains in Rome. I'm sorry, Dad."

"It isn't your fault, Eleanor," he said, putting his arm around me. "You were just being . . . well . . . nice."

"Like I said, big mistake," Solly said again.

"Say that one more time –" I began.

"Come on, you two," my mother stopped me. "The last thing we need is for us to start arguing. Let's think about this tape. Why did Kaspar Snit send it to Solly? He must have wanted to let us know that he was out there. And the letters he sent to you, Manfred, signed by Rapsak T. Ins. He wants us to figure out that he stole the fountains. That's part of his plan for revenge. He wants us to know who's doing this."

"And what do we do now?" Dad asked. "Just this

morning the United Nations declared the disappearance of the fountains to be a world crisis."

It seemed very strange to me – the four of us sitting in Solly's room, trying to figure out what to do about a world crisis. Finally my father said, "There's only one thing to do. Tell the Italian government."

"You can't do that, Daddy," I said.

"I can't see why not."

"Won't the Italian government send their army? And won't Kaspar Snit's army be waiting? There'll be a war."

"Eleanor's right," Mom said. "That's just the sort of destruction that he wants, I bet."

"We'll have to take that chance," my father said. "There just isn't anything else that we can do. Solly, hand me that paper and crayon from your desk. Now hang on a minute. . . ."

We all watched as Dad wrote something on the paper, pausing once to think. "There," he said, putting a final period at the end of the last sentence he had written. "I'll send this E-mail to the Italian government. Eleanor, I heard what you said, but we can't keep this news to ourselves. It's just too enormous. Here, I'll read it to you."

To the president of Italy

The fountains have been stolen by millionaire madman Kaspar Snit. Snit lives in a fortress on Mount Darkling, Verulia. He has a private army and may be hoping to start a war. Approach with extreme caution.

We all agreed that my father had written about as good an E-mail as anyone could. He got up to use the computer in the basement. It was getting late, but my parents let us stay up to wait for the reply. Solly and I got into our pajamas and then my mother gave us a late-night snack of cereal in the kitchen. While we were eating, my father went down to check the computer. He came back up with a sheet of paper in his hand. "This just came," he said, and then read it to us:

To Manfred Blande from the president of Italy

Advisers here do not believe thefts can be the idea of one man. Also, no person is known to inhabit the Verulian Mountains. No doubt foreign countries jealous of Rome's beauty are behind this. All surrounding countries deny involvement, but must be lying. Our army is preparing for war. Time for action, not caution!

"War!" Mom said. "Oh, Manfred, this is terrible. Why won't they believe you?"

"I suppose I can't blame them," Dad said. "It does sound crazy. And if I try to explain that Kaspar Snit stole the fountains because we cooked him a meal, they'll think we're even more crazy. Daisy, this is going to turn out a worse catastrophe than we even imagined. There's going to be war. And there's nothing we can do about it."

Once in bed, I couldn't sleep. Something had to be done, but what? Finally I dozed off. I dreamed that I was a little kid again, lying in my bed, and Kaspar Snit was standing over me with an evil glint in his eye. "*I'll teach you for calling me nice*," he was saying.

When I woke up, shivering, the room was still dark. I pushed off the covers and walked softly down the hall, where, as I somehow knew, I found my mother. The living room window was open, but she wasn't standing before it getting ready to lift off. Instead, she was sitting on the sofa with her chin in her hands.

"Eleanor?" she said, turning. I could just see her eyes, shining in the dark. "You should be asleep."

I sat beside her and she put her arm around my shoulder. "Who would have thought that our nice orderly life could be turned upside down this way."

"Mom," I said. "We have to tell Dad."

"Tell him what?"

"That I know how to fly."

"Honey, your father has more than enough to occupy him at the moment. He hardly needs to hear that."

"But it's the only way. We have to tell him because of the fountains. You see, Mom? We can use our flying. Dad says there aren't any trains, or airplanes, or even roads, into the Verulian Mountains. But you and I can fly there."

"Eleanor, do you know what you're saying? First of all, that's thousands of miles away. It would take days, if we even had the strength. And if we could fly there, what would we do then? Drop rotten eggs on Kaspar Snit's army?"

"No, but we could get proof that he has the fountains, even if we couldn't exactly carry them back."

"I suppose . . ." Mom considered. "And we could get the amulet."

"Hey, that's right."

"It's pretty risky."

We both heard a noise. Turning my head, I saw my father standing in the dark entranceway. His hair was a tousled mess. "What's going on?" he said. "Daisy? You two are up to something."

A moment later Solly appeared behind him, clutching Dad's leg. His messy hair looked like a miniature version of Dad's. "I heard talking," Solly said, rubbing his eyes.

My mother put a hand over her eyes and shook her head. "This is just great."

"Well, Mom?"

She sighed, but then stood up and said, "All right. We had all better go into the yard. Manfred, there's something you and Solly need to see."

She started towards the kitchen. Dad and Solly exchanged puzzled looks, as if to say *we boys never know what's going on*. Then they followed her in single file out the side door, with me bringing up the rear. Solly's walk turned springy. He was happy just to be up so late.

Outside, the night was warm and almost humid. Deep shadows fell over the yard from the surrounding trees. Near the back fence, a lone cricket chirped. Dad and Solly stayed together while I ended up beside my mother, as if we were on two separate teams.

Mom looked at me. "Okay, Eleanor."

I put my arms back, tilted up my chin, and closed my eyes. When I opened them again, I was still on the ground.

"It's all the pressure," I said. "With everyone watching me."

"Go ahead," Mom said. "Clear your mind. Don't try so hard. Just let it happen."

Again I put my arms back and closed my eyes. A long moment passed. I could hear Solly shifting from one foot to another, like he had to go to the bathroom. Dad started to say something, but stopped. A gentle breeze came up. The breeze must have been just the extra help I needed because I could feel myself rising into the air – five, ten, twenty feet. I opened my eyes to see them all looking up at me.

"*Whoa!*" said Solly. "You learned!"

"I should have known this would happen," said Dad. Even in the dark, I could see that his face had turned white. He stalked off towards the house and then, changing his mind, headed for his dormitory office, closing the door behind him. I let myself come back to the ground.

"I was afraid of that," Mom said.

"Eleanor, you are so cool." Solly grinned. "A flying sister. Can I take you to school for show-and-tell? You sure beat Jeremy Worthington with his magic tricks."

"No, no, Solly, you can't tell anybody," Mom said. "I'd better go and speak to your father. Eleanor, you put Solly back to bed and then go to bed yourself. I'm afraid this is going to be a long night."

I did as Mom said, taking Solly back into the house to his room. Obediently he got into bed and I pulled the covers up around him.

"Eleanor?" he said, in the dark.

"Yes, Solly?"

"Are you and Mom, you know, weird or something?"

"I don't think so."

"Is it fun?"

"It's more than fun. It's . . . it's . . ." I remembered a word that my dad had once used about a particularly beautiful fountain with soaring jets of water. "It's sublime."

"Sublime," Solly repeated, feeling the word in his mouth. "Yes, I think that's what it would be. Sublime."

"I hope Mom can convince Dad that flying is a good thing. She has to if we're going to rescue those fountains back from Kaspar Snit."

"We are?" asked Solly. "This gets better every minute."

12

FLYING

FOR BEGINNERS

In the morning I almost whooped for joy to see my father in the kitchen making pancakes. He still looked like he was sulking, but I guessed that he had at least half forgiven my learning to fly. Mom came in next, fixing her blouse and saying, "I'm going to be late for work," and then Solly. My brother wasn't wearing the normal-kid clothes like yesterday. Instead, he was back in his superhero outfit, the flippers going *splonge-splonge* as he walked. Googoo-man was back.

"Morning, Dad," Solly said. "Morning, sis. Morning, Googoo-*mom*."

"Very funny," Mom said. "Now listen, kids. I want you to have a normal day at school and then come right home.

Eleanor, you've got to get your homework done and then both of you need a rest."

"That's right," Dad said, piling our plates with pancakes. "We're going to be up late tonight."

"Up late?" I said.

"Mom told me about your plan, Eleanor. And I can't think of anything better. We'll take a camera with us and photograph the fountains as proof for the Italian government."

"We?" I said. "But only Mom and I can fly. You and Solly don't have the amulet marks."

"That's true at the moment," Mom said. She opened her palm and looked at it. "But I know a way."

"I'm going to learn to fly, I'm going to learn to fly!" Solly cried.

My father looked at my brother, springing up and down and making a racket. "I think I regret it already," he said.

The school day felt like the longest in my life. First we had a math quiz, which I must have got, maybe, one right answer on. Then Julia Worthington presented us with her homemade weather station, smacking me in the back of the head with the wind vane as she came up the aisle. After that, Mr. Bentham decided to give us one of his off-the-cuff lectures, while sitting on top of the file cabinet. Usually I liked Mr. Bentham's lectures; they were full of unusual and interesting information on things like the development of the sandwich, or that the word "hello" was invented by Alexander Graham Bell to give people something to say

when they picked up the telephone. But today I didn't hear
a word Mr. Bentham said. I guess thinking about how you
and your family have to save the world from war can make
it hard to concentrate.

After school, I met Solly at his classroom door and we
raced home together. We wanted to talk about what was
going to happen tonight, but Mom and Dad told us that we
had to finish the day like it was any other. So I had to go and
do my homework and then we had dinner, when nobody
said just about anything. After that, Solly took his bath,
protesting as always when my mother washed his hair, and
I took a shower. Then came reading time and lights out.

"You get some sleep," Mom said to me as she kissed me
good night. "We'll tell you when it's time to get up."

Sleep? How could I possibly sleep? There was no way. . . .

"Time to get up, Eleanor." It was my father, gently shaking
my shoulder. *Huh*? I guessed that I really had fallen asleep.
Dad said, "We've got work to do."

I saw that he had our camera slung around his neck.
Oh, yes, he had to take pictures of the fountains. "What
time is it?" I asked.

"Ten at night. You were asleep only an hour. We need as
many night hours as possible. Come on."

I sprang out of bed. Outside my window it was dark. In
the hallway we met my mom and Solly, who naturally had
on his Googoo-man costume. He was carrying a plastic
grocery bag. My parents flipped on an outside light and
led us through the kitchen out into the backyard.

"Mom, I still don't see how Solly and Dad can fly without the amulet. They don't have the markings."

"We have to give them the markings. My grandmother told me about this, but I've never tried it. Solly, Manfred, hold out your open hands. All right, Eleanor. You do Solly and I'll do Dad. Take your palm and press it hard against Solly's for a good minute."

I opened my hand and looked at the moon and three stars. The blue had lightened a little in the last twenty-four hours and I guessed that it would be completely faded away in another five or six days. Solly was standing in front of me and eagerly holding out his hand. I saw Mom take Dad's and so I reached out to steady Solly's wrist with one hand while pressing my palm down into his.

"Don't squirm, Solly!"

"But it hurts!"

"I have to do it hard."

Soon my mother said, "That ought to be enough," before letting go of my father's hand. I waited another second or two and released Solly's. He paused a minute and then turned his hand over so that we could see his palm under the light.

"It's there!" he shrieked.

Yes it was, the moon and stars, only in reverse, on Solly's palm. Dad had it too.

"I feel a little weird," Dad said.

"Trust me, it gets worse." I turned over my hand and looked at my own palm. The markings were still there, but so faded that I gasped in dismay.

"That's right," Mom said, on hearing me. "Mine are faded too. Our markings will last only half the amount of time now. I would guess that we've all got about three days of flying, only enough to get there. We'll just have to hope that we can get the amulet back and imprint ourselves for the return trip. Manfred, you've got film in the camera and new batteries, right?"

"Right," said Dad.

"Eleanor, we've got to give these boys their wings. Let's teach them to fly."

"Yes!" Solly said, pumping the air with his puny fist. "We're going to whip that Kaspar Snit's butt."

"Keep your voice down, Solly," Dad said. "The neighbors will hear. Besides, I'm hoping that I can just have a little talk with Rapsak – I mean, Kaspar – and convince him to give the fountains back."

"Really, Dad." Solly tapped one swim flipper impatiently. "You can't negotiate with the Prince of Darkness."

"First things first," Mom said. "And the first step is getting off the ground. Eleanor, you're going to be Solly's coach. I'll help Dad. First we'll show them the right position. Look at my feet, my legs, and my arms. Manfred, your hands are tilted the wrong way. That's better. But position is only the beginning. The most important thing is –"

"Your state of mind," I cut in.

"Right. Now listen closely."

I listened too as my mother began to instruct Solly and Dad in the fine art of thinking like a flyer. Solly listened with his mouth hanging open and his eyes wide. I have to say that he looked pretty dumb. Frowning, my father concentrated hard, though he looked as if he couldn't believe what my mother was telling him. "All right," she said finally, an almost military snap to her voice. "Let's get in position."

"Wait," Solly said. "I brought something for everybody."

We watched him reach into the plastic grocery bag that he had left on the ground. He pulled out a fistful of towels. And then, with the other hand, goggles.

"What's that for?" I asked.

"If we're all going to be superheroes and go around flying, I think we ought to look the part. Now I don't have full costumes for all of you, but I do have goggles and capes."

"Solly, that's ridiculous," Dad growled. "We're doing something serious here."

"I *know* it's serious. That's why you have to look the part. Kaspar Snit won't want to mess with a whole family of superheroes. You'll see. Besides, the goggles will keep dust and stuff out of your eyes."

Dad looked at Mom, who shrugged. "Who knows?" she said. "Maybe he's right."

"Here, Eleanor." Solly handed me a towel cape and a pair of goggles. "These are for you. And here, Dad. Mom, these are yours."

Reluctantly, we all put on our gear and then looked at one another. Solly was as happy as I'd ever seen him. "Look at us!" he said. "Googoo-dad, Googoo-mom, Googoo-sis, and Googoo-man. The invincible four!"

"Shouldn't you be called Googoo-*boy*?" I asked.

"Watch it," Solly said. "Remember that I'm the only one with a sonic blaster and a neutronic knocker."

"You mean, a bicycle horn and a sock filled with guck."

"That's enough," Mom said, fluffing out her cape behind her. Hers said DRINK SHNELL'S ROOT BEER on it. "Time is running short. We have only a few hours of flying time since we'll be moving towards the sun and have to land before it gets light out. Arms back, everybody. Fingers together. Hands at thirty degrees. Chin up, eyes closed. Feel the lift in the balls of your feet. Think flying. I'll count to ten. Ready? One . . . two . . . three. . . ."

I gave Solly an encouraging look and he smiled and flashed me a quick salute. I kind of liked wearing the cape – mine said TWO FREE RUMBA LESSONS! – and it was true that the goggles might be useful. Now I closed my own eyes and, as my mother reached "ten," I felt myself rise into the air some twenty-five feet. I was getting better at judging height, speed, direction, and distance. When I opened my eyes, I saw only my mother hovering across from me.

"Hey!" came Solly's voice from below. I looked down to see him and my father staring up at us, both of them with their hands indignantly on their hips. "Not fair," Solly said. "It didn't work."

My mother rolled her eyes. "Boys," she said. "They take twice as long to learn anything. We'd better go down and try again."

The two of us landed back in our places. "I feel like an idiot," my father said. "I might as well start hooting like an owl."

"Maybe that's part of the problem, Manfred," Mom said. "You have the wrong attitude. Now come on, you've got to try again. Just remember why we're doing this. This time, really free your mind. If you don't let go of your disbelief, you won't get anywhere. Try and *hear* flying in your mind."

"Hear?" Dad said. "You mean *vroom-vroom*, like a jet engine?"

"Dad," I said, "that isn't trying."

"Okay, okay."

"Here we go," Mom said, trying to inject some enthusiasm. "Assume your positions. One . . . two . . . three . . . four. . . ."

Once more I closed my eyes and once more I felt myself rise into the night sky. This time I opened my eyes and saw – Solly! His nose was about half an inch from my own.

"Hey, it works!"

"Well, give me some space," I said, treading backwards.

"Good for you, Solly," my mother said. "I knew you could do it."

Solly was so excited that he did a full somersault in the air, making my mother and me scream.

"What's the problem?" he asked, right-side-up again. "It's easy."

"Don't show off, Solly. You aren't experienced yet."

"If you say so," Solly said, and then did a fast 360 degree twirl, his cape whirling around him.

"Maybe we should have kept it to ourselves," I said.

"*Ahem*, did you forget about *me*?" came a voice from below.

"Oh, sorry, honey," Mom said, looking down. And there was my father, alone this time and looking positively annoyed at the fact. From here I could see how his hair was getting thin on top, but I thought it better not to point it out at this particular moment.

Dad began to flap his arms and jump up and down. "I . . . can't . . . get . . . up!" he whined. Well, who ever heard of taking off that way?

"Okay, crew," Mom said, winking at Solly and me. "Let's go help the landlubber down there."

We *tried* to help. We did everything we could possibly think of to get my father into the air, short of flinging him from a catapult. But even with the imprint from the amulet, he just didn't have the talent for it. All the while he became more and more frustrated. "Come on, Dad, it's *so easy*," Solly said, not helping matters much. At last even my mother had to concede defeat.

"The simple fact is, not everyone can fly," she said. "But then most people can't design fountains either, Manfred." I wondered if he knew all along that he wouldn't have the knack for it. Maybe that was the real reason he had never tried.

The four of us sat on the back porch steps, our hands in our chins. Every so often Solly would get up to fly again and my mother would yank him back down by his cape.

"This is just great," Dad said, his goggles crooked. "Now we'll never get to Kaspar Snit's fortress."

"Wait," I said. "We can still go."

"How?" Mom asked.

"We'll just carry Dad along with us. He can hold on to our hands."

"I will not!"

"I don't know," Mom said. "It'll be tiring. We've got farther to go than you or I have ever flown before, Eleanor."

"But I know we can do it, Mom."

"Am I part of this discussion?" Dad said. "I have no intention of being dragged through the sky."

Mom stood up. "This is no time to be proud. Do you want to save civilization or not? Let's give it a try. We don't have another minute of darkness to lose."

13

TRAVEL
BY NIGHT

The problem was that holding my father's hands didn't work either. My mother and I had an awful time getting up into the air and, when we finally did – rising like an elephant swimming up through water – it was just too hard to maneuver. After only a couple of minutes, we spiraled slowly back to the ground, the three of us landing in a heap.

"That looks like fun," Solly said. "Can I jump on too?"

We were just about defeated when my mother had an idea. In the basement we had a leather harness and leash that Solly had insisted we buy last summer at the Worthingtons' garage sale. The Worthingtons had owned a dog for about a month, but Jeremy Worthington kept sneaking up on it and shouting "Boo!" and Julia Worthington kept dressing it up in her old clothes and the dog started to become neurotic. This meant that every time Julia or Jeremy came near it, the poor thing made this awful noise like it had a chicken bone stuck in its throat. So Mr. Worthington found a nice farmer who wanted a dog, and now it was much happier living with cows and chickens than it had been with the Worthington kids.

Solly had wanted the old harness and leash. He was hoping that his friend Ginger Hirshbein would consent to wear it and pretend to be a dog so that Googoo-man could have a faithful companion. But although Ginger didn't mind being rescued over and over again, he didn't want to become a dog. So the harness had been relegated to the basement. Mom ran and got it and, although Dad backed away muttering, "Oh, no, you don't," she and I managed to get it on him. A few strap adjustments and it fit snugly. Then we snapped a leash on it for Mom to hold and a leather strap from an old purse for me.

"I don't like this one bit," Dad said.

"Relax, Manfred. Just enjoy the ride."

Getting up still wasn't easy, but once we were airborne with Dad trailing close behind us, the drag made flying only a little harder.

Solly took off and flew next to us. "Hey, it's Cargo Dad."

"Do not call me that," Dad grumbled. Mom and I tried not to snicker.

So there we were, all of us with our goggles over our eyes and towel capes fluttering behind. "To Verulia – and victory!" Solly called out in his deepest voice. Soon we found a formation that suited us best, with Solly in the lead so that the rest of us could keep an eye on him, then Mom and me side by side behind him, and Dad in the harness trailing just behind and below us. Solly honked his sonic blaster at a formation of Canada geese, who began honking back, and once my father complained that we were going too fast, but after an hour or so everyone became quiet and we concentrated on our flying.

It felt strange to be going farther and farther away from home, knowing that we weren't going to turn around and be back before morning. Dad told us when we reached the Quebec border, after which we followed the coastline of the Saint Lawrence River. Sometimes it was dark below and sometimes there were the lights of a town, and then the river opened up into the wide Gulf of Saint Lawrence. It was windier and colder over the water and I felt myself shiver. Mom was worried about Solly getting tired, and every so often she would call out to him. At first he kept calling back, "Look up in the air! It's Googoo-man!" and then, after a while, just "Okay, Mom," and finally he would only nod his head, like he was trying to save energy. The sky began to turn from black to gray and I was glad to see an island coast appear up ahead.

"There's Newfoundland," Mom said. "We'll stop there for the day. Okay, Solly, let's start a gentle descent."

"Roger, traffic control," Solly said.

And then something happened. I felt a pull and a sort of *twang*, like an elastic breaking, and suddenly I was shooting ahead past Solly. It took me a moment to realize that the strap between me and my father had broken. I heard a yell and, turning back, saw him zinging back and forth below my mother as he dangled from the single leash. Mom struggled to keep aloft, but the weight and swinging movement of my father was causing her to jerk downwards. If she went into a nosedive, both she and Dad would plunge straight into the waters of the Cabot Strait.

"Solly!" I called out, even as I soared towards my father. His face was whiter than chalk.

"Eleanor!" Dad cried. "Unlatch the leash. Save your mother!"

But I had another idea. I flew directly under my father and rose gradually up, taking as much of his weight on my back as I could. Mom was still losing height, but not so quickly, and she started to regain some control. Solly had finally circled back and now he hovered beside me, his eyes big with fear.

"What should I do?" he shouted.

"Tie the broken strap," I said. "And hurry. I don't think I can make it to the coast."

"I'm not very good at knots yet," Solly said.

"Then you support Dad and I'll do it."

"It won't work," Dad said. "You have to cut me loose, Eleanor."

"That's not an option, Manfred" came my mother's voice from above us. Solly took my place, gasping as he carried some of Dad's weight. I did a quick maneuver to get above my father, but because I couldn't fly and use my hands at the same time, I had to sit on him. Solly gasped even louder and we sank closer to the ocean waves. My hands fumbled the leather ends but finally I tied the knot, pulling it as tight as I could.

"I think I got it."

"Are you sure?" Mom asked.

"I don't know."

There was nothing to do but find out. Solly eased away from my father and I felt the strap strain against my wrist as I rose from his back. There was a moment when the knot suddenly tightened, but it held and I moved beside my mother again, just a little behind her because my strap was shorter now.

Mom looked at me with an exhausted smile. "Let's go down," she said.

I was never so glad to feel the earth under my feet. We took off our capes and goggles, all except Solly, and rested awhile in a grove of stunted trees. Then we walked down a path that took us to a small fishing village. The sun was just rising, giving the clapboard houses a pink hue. Small boats rocked in the waters of the cove. Up early, the fishermen were checking their nets. One and then another turned on his motor and began chugging out to deeper water.

We walked to the dock where a boy sat fishing, his legs dangling over the edge. He had a baseball cap pulled down tight on his head, with red hair sticking out from under it. His rubber boots looked about ten sizes too big. Dad said, "Hi there, young fellow. Is there a hotel nearby?"

The boy squinted up at us. "Not around here," he said. "You'd have to go into Cornerbrook for that, must be seventy miles. Of course, there's Mrs. Macready. She lets rooms. Makes a nice breakfast too. Third house up from the dock."

"That's fine," Dad said. "I don't suppose there's a pet shop around here?"

The boy's squint narrowed. "You want to buy a pet? I got a guinea pig you can have for a dollar. He's real nice. Only thing is, he's missing one leg. But I fixed him with a wooden one and he walks just fine. Makes a clicking sound."

"No," Dad said, "we just need a leash."

"You have a dog?"

"*Ah*, not actually."

"Thinking of getting one someday?"

"Yes, that's it. We're thinking of getting one."

"Well, there's no pet shop around here."

"I see. Well, thanks for your help, son. All right, everyone, let's see if Mrs. Macready has room for us."

My father and mother started walking up the path. Solly and I lingered behind and kept looking at the boy, who kept squinting up at us. A mutual fascination, I guessed. Solly said, "How did your guinea pig lose his leg?"

"Car accident."

"Your guinea pig drives a car?" Solly said.

The boy jerked his fishing line and then looked back at us. "I saw something this morning. In the sky. Saw *four* somethings."

My heart began to beat fast. "What do you mean? Geese, maybe?"

"Too big for geese. Way too big. What are you supposed to be, anyway?" he said to Solly, eyeing his Googoo-man costume.

"What?" I said. "That outfit? Oh, we're on our way to a Halloween party, aren't we, Solly?"

"Yeah, that's right."

The boy turned back to his rod. "May is kind of early for a Halloween party. Six months early."

"Didn't you hear?" I said. "They changed the date. So the weather would be better."

The boy pulled up his rod and peered at his hook, as if unconvinced that it was still there. A bit of soggy bread was stuck on it. He lowered the line again.

"Don't worry," he said. "I'm not planning on telling anybody. They wouldn't believe me anyway."

"Thanks," I said. Just then my father called us from up the path.

"That's okay."

We started walking after our parents. Solly said to me, "They changed the date for Halloween?"

At the house before Mrs. Macready's, there was a dog-house below the porch. Not just for show either; there was a dog half in and half out of it, chewing on the largest bone I had ever seen, like it was from a triceratops, or something. But it was the right size for such a large and mean-looking dog, which stared at us with glassy eyes as we went by. Luckily for us, it was chained to a stake by the doghouse.

"Look," Solly said. "There's a leash." Solly was right; a leash hung from a nail on the front of the doghouse, a strong-looking one too. "Good doggy," said Solly.

The dog raised its head from the bone. A low growl started from deep in its throat. It showed its very large canine teeth.

"Don't even think about it, Solly," I said.

Mrs. Macready had a pretty clapboard house, with blue shingles and pots of daisies on either side of the door. Both her rooms were available for us and if she thought it strange that my mother ordered us to bed right after breakfast, she didn't say so. So while everyone else in the village was beginning a new day, the four of us were getting into bed and pulling feather quilts up to our chins. I was asleep almost before my head touched the pillow.

14

THE STORM

We got up at dinnertime, refreshed from our long sleep and hungry again, which made the smells from Mrs. Macready's kitchen even more irresistible. We sat at the table while Mrs. Macready heaped up our plates with roast chicken, mashed potatoes, and fiddleheads, and told us about her sons, grown up and living in the city, and how the fish were running and how the school needed a new roof. I knew what my mother would say – that she was talking so much because she was lonely from living alone. She had a very old radio sitting on the sideboard, which was playing music – I had a feeling she kept it on all day long – and when the news came on, we all stopped to listen.

Meanwhile, on the international scene, there is more bad news from Italy. With all the fountains now stolen from the once-great city of Rome, the government has declared a state of war. Who exactly the country is at war with is uncertain, but as soldiers are put on alert and airplanes and tanks made ready, surrounding countries are feeling threatened. Foreign ministers are denouncing these actions as "aggressive" and "provocative" and are putting their own armies on high alert. A special session of the United Nations has been called for tomorrow morning. . . .

Mrs. Macready snapped off the radio. "Terrible, terrible," she said, clicking her tongue. "You know, Mr. Macready and I had planned to go to Rome one day and see the fountains. But we were always too busy. Now that I have time, my sister and I were going to go this summer. I wanted to throw a coin in the Trevi Fountain in memory of my dear George. But there's no sense in going now, with those fountains all gone and everybody talking about war. What is the world coming to? Well, it's enough to make you lose faith in humankind."

My mother told Mrs. Macready not to give up on her trip to Rome just yet, but Mrs. Macready didn't seem to feel much hope and I could see how her words made my father more somber. Until that moment, I hadn't understood that those fountains meant something even to people who had never seen them. We thanked Mrs. Macready for her hospitality and paid the bill. Then we followed the path as darkness fell, Mrs. Macready waving to us from her porch.

We walked back down to the cove, deserted now but for the boats bobbing in the water, where they were anchored. The dock smelled of fish, but it had been washed down and was damp under our shoes. I couldn't help glancing at my palm and noticing that the moon and stars had become a pale yellow. Mom said, "All right, crew. Tonight we have to be especially careful. We're crossing the Atlantic Ocean. There'll be no land in sight for most of the trip and nowhere to put down until we reach France. If my calculations are correct, we're going to have to fly the last hours in daylight. So let's keep a good pace and have no fooling around. The air over the Atlantic can get rough in spots, so you'll need all your wits. You hear me, Solly?"

"I hear you, Mom."

Dad said, "I was thinking of not wearing my goggles and cape."

"*Aw*, Dad!" said Solly.

"But they look so silly. I feel foolish enough in that harness."

"Come on, Dad. Please. How can we be a superhero family if you don't wear them?"

"Oh, all right."

"Thanks, Dad."

"Oh, we forgot," I said. "My strap broke. We didn't get a new one."

"That's right." Mom examined the old strap with the knot we had made. "There's no way this is going to hold for the whole trip. And it would be too dangerous to try. But we've got to take advantage of the dark while we can."

"I have an idea," Solly said. "Hang on a minute."

"Solly, don't –" I cried after him, remembering the mean dog in the doghouse. But it was too late. He zoomed up the path, disappearing over the little hill. A moment later we heard a growl, bark, and snap, followed by Solly's "*yowch!*" Then Solly was speeding down the path again, the leash in his hand.

"Here," he said, trying to catch his breath. "Use this."

My mother gave Solly a good stare, but attached the leash to the harness. It was then I noticed a ripped flap of Solly's bathing suit and pajamas hanging down at the back, exposing his underpants. I used one of the safety pins from my cape to fix it. "Solly," I said. "That dog almost got you!"

"Well," he smiled at me, "I'm glad it was 'almost.'"

We got into position and my mother started the countdown. Getting my father into the air was, if anything, harder because my muscles felt sore today, but soon we were flying over the ocean at a steady pace – high enough so as not to be spotted by any ships and low enough to see the moonlight glinting on the waves. We flew for two or three hours without speaking much but then Solly started to complain of getting sleepy, so my father told him to fly closer while he told us about Rome. Even though Solly and I had been born there, I could remember only a little and Solly could remember nothing at all. He told us how two thousand years ago Rome needed water, so the Romans began to build aqueducts. These aqueducts, which were really clay pipes, brought water to the city from rivers that were miles and miles away. When they got to the city they fed into the fountains, where people could come with their pots and buckets to take the water they needed for drinking, cooking, and washing.

Dad kept Solly and me alert with his descriptions. I felt even more sorry that the fountains were gone. Listening so closely to him, we had hardly noticed the growing turbulence in the air, or that the moon had disappeared. But then suddenly the air turned rough, bumping and rocking us as we flew.

"Hey, I don't like this!" Solly said.

"Keep calm," Mom said. "Solly, you stay beside us. Just ride with the bumps, don't fight them. Eleanor, are you all right?"

"I think so," I said, trying to hide the fear that had jumped inside me and was twisting in my stomach. I felt as if someone were slapping and punching me. I had the strap of the dog leash around my wrist and it yanked and wrenched at my hand as my father bounced back and forth between my mother and me. A raindrop hit me in the eye, making me blink. A moment later an onslaught of rain came down, soaking me instantly and pouring down my face so that I could barely see, even with the goggles on.

"Hang on!" shouted my mother. "Eleanor, are you okay?"

"Okay!" I shouted.

"Solly?"

There was no answer, just the pounding of the rain on my body and the wind roaring in my ears.

"Solly!" my father shouted. "SOLLY!"

I heard a faint sound and realized what it was – Googoo-man's sonic blaster. He had been driven somewhere far down below. The storm was pushing him away from us.

There was nothing for us to do but keep flying, my mother and father and I calling out Solly's name. But there was no reply. After a while the rain began to let up; we were moving out of the storm. The air became smooth and I could see the moon, round and bright over the calm ocean. My wet clothes stuck to my body. But I couldn't feel relieved because Solly, my little brother, was gone.

For a long moment, nobody said anything. "It's my fault," Mom said finally. "I should never have taught him how to fly. He was too young. Oh, Manfred."

"It's my fault," said Dad. "I should never have agreed to do this. I put the fountains before my own family."

But I knew they were both wrong. It was my fault because it was my idea. I thought flying to the Verulian Mountains would be just a big adventure. Well, how wrong I was. And now there was nothing I could do about it.

A sound. It came from far away, somewhere down below and to the left. I heard it again, three times. It sounded like a Canada goose that had got separated from its formation in the storm. The honking got louder and closer. And then I realized that it wasn't a goose at all.

"It's the sonic blaster!" I cried. "It's Solly!"

And there he was, visible below us and getting larger as he rose. "Oh, my dear Solly!" Mom said, and started to cry. Dad began to wave frantically at him, so that Mom and I had to tell him to quit it before we went into a spin. We all waited as Solly came up alongside, drenched as we were but otherwise unharmed.

"Wow, what a ride!" Solly said. "I got knocked right down to the sea. A dolphin saved me."

"Solly," Mom said. "You've had enough of an adventure without having to make things up."

"I mean it. I went right into the water and the dolphin came up under me so that I could hold on to its back. It kept me above water. Let me tell you, it wasn't easy taking off while standing on a slippery back."

"I think we should turn around," my father said. "I don't want to put the kids at risk another minute."

"It would take longer to go back than to keep going, Manfred. Look at the horizon. It's turning orange. The sun is starting to come up. We'll be at the coast of France in another hour."

The storm had pushed us farther south than we had intended to go, and we landed on a beach north of the resort town of Biarritz. Luckily, the couple walking at the end of the beach had their backs turned as we landed, but they looked awfully surprised to turn again and see four people suddenly appear from nowhere, all of them in goggles and capes and one of them (my father) lying on his stomach. He got up, going "*phut-phut-phut*" to get the sand out of his mouth.

Just up from the beach was a small hotel and once again we took rooms, ate a meal, and headed for bed. Our clothes had already dried from the air while we flew, but Mom washed out some of our things and hung them up to be fresh for morning – or rather evening, when we got up again. I slept so heavily that my parents had to spend ten minutes gently shaking me awake, but then I was up and dressed in no time.

Since it was our morning, even if the sun was going down, my father asked the hotel if they might serve us breakfast. The waiter looked at us like we were very strange foreigners indeed, but he brought deliciously buttery croissants, sugary rolls, and bowls of café au lait (well, only a drop of coffee in ours).

My father bit into a jam-covered croissant. "I think we should go home," he said. "By regular airplane. This trip is turning out to be too dangerous. Look what happened to Solly – we almost lost him."

"But, Dad," Solly said, "we've already crossed the ocean. We've got to get that evil Kaspar Snit. I know we can do it."

"It is true that we've come this far," Mom said. "I'm so proud of our kids, Manfred. They've been very brave."

"Of course we should be proud," said Dad. "But they are still kids, Daisy."

"Think of the fountains, Dad," I said. "And think of what would happen if a war breaks out. We'd be in danger then too, wouldn't we? And so would the rest of the world. We have to take those photographs and prove that Kaspar Snit stole those fountains. And we have to get back the amulet. I think we should go on."

"Eleanor's right, Manfred."

My dad looked first at my mom, then at Solly, and finally
at me. He wiped his mouth with his napkin and stood up.
"You're all in agreement?"

"Yes," Solly said.

"Yes," I said.

"Yes, Manfred," my mother said.

"All right then, let's make it unanimous."

"What does 'you-nanny-moose' mean?" asked Solly.

"It means we're going to get Kaspar Snit," I said.

"Yes!"

"But let's take no unnecessary risks," Dad went on. "I
want you kids well away from any danger."

"Googoo-girl laughs in the face of danger," I said.

"Googoo-girl better listen to her father," Dad warned.
"Or she'll be going to bed early for the rest of her life."

15

TO VERULIA!

This last night of flying had different dangers, for we had to cross over no less than five countries. Some of these countries were suspicious of one another at the best of times and kept their military at the ready, but the crisis over the disappearing fountains had put all the countries of Europe on high alert. If their radar picked us up, we might be identified as enemy planes or missiles and an attack launched upon us.

Dad thought that we would have a better chance of avoiding detection by flying low and avoiding the big cities, so we had to take a meandering route, flying over fields, canals, railway tracks, factories, highways, and forests. All of us turned our thoughts to the destination ahead – the mountain on which Kaspar Snit had built his fortress. And as the night deepened and midnight came and then seemed far behind us, we all became afraid for what lay ahead.

My father knew a pass through the Carpathian Mountains and I found it a greater and greater effort to keep going. I had to force my mind to concentrate, while my legs began to tremble. Finally I realized what was happening: the amulet marks on my palm were fading away. Nobody else seemed to be having the same trouble yet, so I didn't say anything and just forced myself to focus even harder.

It was Mom who realized first that we had reached the foothills of the Verulian Mountains. Dad took a small compass out of his pocket and pointed the direction for us to follow. We skirted the mountain range's edge for several miles until Dad said, "That way, up that route. It leads to the top of Mount Darkling."

And so we began to climb, flying upwards, parallel to the rising ground. The drag caused by pulling my father became a lot more tiring as the way became more steep. Now there were no thatched-roofed cottages or pens of goats, but only rocks and bushes and streams tumbling down, and we kept going up and up so far that I thought we would never reach the top.

"Holy cow," said Solly.

I looked up and saw what he meant. There was Kaspar Snit's fortress, so forbidding that it terrified me just to look at it.

The fortress was made of enormous stone blocks and the surrounding wall rose fifty feet high. At the corner I could see a round stone tower and the shadow of a guard inside. The site of the fortress was so cold and cruel that it made me tremble. Mom whispered for us to keep going, so we rose up alongside the wall and then, as we neared the top, she hissed, "Don't stop!" and we continued until we were hovering above the fortress, hidden by the dark.

"I feel a little dizzy," I said.

"The air is thin," said Dad. "Take slow, deep breaths. We've got to figure out our next move."

I knew it wasn't the air, but the fading marks on my palm. The four of us looked down into the fortress. The walls enclosed a space as big as four football fields. Near one end, looking as if it didn't belong there, was a mansion of a house. My mother said it was in the style of a French château and I had to admit it was very elegant. At the other end was a plain wooden building that my father said must be the barracks for Kaspar Snit's army. And between the two of them were the fountains.

Hundreds and hundreds of fountains, all gleaming in the moonlight. There were huge fountains with marble goddesses and gods and creatures that were half human, half animal. There were sea serpents and dolphins and columns and arches, big fountains and not so big, all the way down to the smallest corner fountains with no names. "Look, there's the Trevi Fountain!" my father said, pointing to one of the biggest. "And there's the Leaky Boat! They're all here."

The fountains were silent and still; without their sprays and jets and falls of water they looked frozen in time. I could also see ten black helicopters that had been used to lift the fountains from their places. But my head felt woozy and the fountains and helicopters began to blur.

"See there!" Solly cried. "In the corner. That's *our* fountain!"

Yes, there it was. How forlorn it looked, sitting against one of the stone walls. It really did belong in front of our house. As I gazed at it, I began to feel my eyelids flutter.

"Manfred, can you take a photograph?" said Mom.

My father grabbed the camera that had been hanging from his neck and looked through the viewfinder. "It's too dark," he said. "And we're too high up for the flash to be effective. We'll have to land so that I can get closer and hope that the guards won't notice us."

"And then," said my mother, "we'll have to reach our fountain and get back the amulet. Our markings are faded almost to nothing."

"I think mine might already be nothing," I said. "I'm really, really, dizzy." At that moment, I could feel my own eyes roll up.

"ELEANOR!"

I couldn't see anything but somehow I knew that I was plunging downwards, dragging my father and mother along with me. And then I must have lost consciousness because the next thing I knew, I was lying on the ground, my head in my mother's lap and my father rubbing my hands and saying, "Eleanor, can you hear us? Eleanor!"

"What . . . what happened?" I asked, opening my eyes and trying to sit up.

"Careful there," Dad said. "Solly and Mom got a hold of you. We all came down with a bit of a thump. Can you get up, Eleanor?"

"I think so." My legs felt wobbly, but my parents helped me up and I managed to stand. "Is everybody else all right?" I said.

"Sure," Solly said. "We're hunky-dory."

"*How glad I am to hear it.*"

It was that voice — that deep, frightening voice on the cassette tape in Solly's room. We all turned to see a very tall man with yellowish skin in the moonlight. He had a little pointed black beard, gleaming eyes, and he wore a long black cape. His smile was the most cruel I had ever seen.

"The evil Kaspar Snit!" Solly yelped.

"At your service." Kaspar Snit bowed from the waist, flourishing his cape. "How delighted I am to be able to show you a little of our local hospitality."

He clapped his hands twice. A low rumble like the sound of thunder arose and I realized it was the pounding of feet. In a moment, two rows of soldiers encircled us. They were dressed in long gray coats, metal helmets, heavy boots, and each carried a wooden pike topped by a curving blade.

"Drat," said Solly. "We're outnumbered."

"Before these gentlemen show you to your quarters," said Kaspar Snit, "I have one question. Where have you put your parachutes?"

"Parachutes?" Dad repeated.

"Yes, the parachutes you used to drop in here. Obviously

you have jumped from an airplane. The guards in the tower should have seen you. At this very moment they are undergoing, shall we say, corrective instruction. Now, where are those parachutes?"

"We didn't use parachutes, you insect," Solly said. "We flew."

"Solly, be polite," Mom said, casting a worried glance at Kaspar Snit. But Kaspar Snit only smiled – a sneer of a smile.

"Ah, so this is our superhero, is it? In green pajamas, I see. What is the name again? Googoo-runt?"

"Googoo-man!"

"Perhaps it should be Googoo-crybaby."

"He's just trying to rile you, Solly," I whispered.

"The rest of you look equally ridiculous in those goggles and capes. But you did not answer my question, Manfred," Kaspar Snit said, the smile disappearing from his face as he turned back to my father. "Those parachutes. I see you still have the harness on, although it's not one I've ever seen before. I wouldn't want you finding some use for those parachutes, like tying them together and using them to escape over the wall. Now tell me where they are before I resort to less friendly measures."

"Well . . ." my father hesitated.

"We ate them," I blurted out.

"You *ate* them?" He raised a sceptical eyebrow.

"Yes, they were experimental parachutes made out of spun sugar. Sort of like cotton candy. They're a new development of the space program."

"In that case you won't be hungry for some time. Guards!"

The soldiers took a step closer, pounding their pikes on the earth. "Captain, let's show the Blandes a good old-fashioned Verulian welcome. Throw them into the dungeon!"

Solly narrowed his eyes and said, "No dungeon has ever been able to hold Googoo-man."

Kaspar Snit turned his small black eyes on my brother. They were cold and glassy, like the eyes of a lizard. "There's a first time for everything," he said. He turned on the heels of his shiny black boots and strode away.

As the soldiers marched us to a heavy wooden door in one of the fortress walls, I tried to talk myself out of being scared. After all, wasn't a dungeon really just a basement with a few extras? They were both underground, they both could be damp, and both had spiders in them. All right, a basement usually had a Ping-Pong table and a dungeon had chains bolted to the walls for holding prisoners. And in a dungeon, there was always the sound of water going *drip, drip, drip*, and moss and ooze and the fluttering of bats' wings overhead and maybe a pile of bones in a corner. Otherwise, they were identical.

One of the soldiers opened the wooden door behind which was a dank stone stairway lit by candles. The stairway seemed to go down forever, but finally we came to another door, this one with a window of iron bars. The captain, who had a long bristly mustache and a fierce scowl, unlocked it with an enormous key and hurried us in. According to my own definition, Kaspar Snit had the perfect dungeon. It had everything – chains, moss, ooze, the *drip, drip, drip*, and even a pile of bones. The only light came from an iron grate high above us. The captain bolted the door and the soldiers marched back up again.

"You can't just leave us here!" my father called to their retreating footsteps. And then, more quietly, "At least, I don't think so."

"Let's not panic." Mom sat on a stone step. She had already taken off her goggles but now she undid her cape. Dad and I took ours off too. "There must be a way out."

"That's simple," Solly said. He walked up to the bolted door and from his belt took the neutronic knocker. Now he walloped the sock against the door. Nothing.

"That's strange," Solly said. "There must be a force field."

"Or maybe," I said, "a wooden door two feet thick is stronger than a sock."

"That's enough, you two," Mom said. "Time for you both to get some rest. We're all tired. That straw looks dry. Go on, now, and close your eyes."

Reluctantly, Solly and I lay down on the straw. It so happened that I was allergic to straw and immediately began to sneeze. Within two minutes I could hear Solly's slow breathing. My father went to sit beside my mother. They kept their voices low, but I could still hear.

"It's him, all right," Dad said. "I remember how tall and thin he was. And that voice is unmistakable. But he wasn't so, well, creepy. I felt sorry for him then. He seemed so lonely."

"He *was* lonely," Mom said. "And you did a good thing, bringing him to our little apartment that night. He could have used the experience differently, to see how it was possible to be happy. Instead, he became resentful and jealous. That's his doing, not ours."

"I suppose so. I can't make out what he's going to do with us."

"He probably doesn't know. It's not as if he was expecting visitors to drop in. Let's hope that there's something other than evil left inside him."

"I hope so, Daisy. But I didn't see it when he looked at me. Well, we'd better have a rest too." They lay down on the stone step and Dad put his arm around Mom. I was surprised to hear him chuckle quietly. "We *ate* our parachutes. Honestly. The things kids think of. . . ."

I was abruptly awakened by a banging sound. Opening my eyes, I saw the captain running the end of his pike across the bars of the door.

"Get up! Get up!" he commanded. "The evil Kaspar Snit requests your presence at lunch."

Slowly we roused ourselves, Solly and I pulling straw out of our hair. The soldiers marched us single file up the long stairs. My father whispered, "Even the soldiers call him the *evil* Kaspar Snit. It's like an advertising slogan, or a brand name. How arrogant can he be?"

"No talking!" the captain shouted.

At that Solly reached down and gave the rubber ball of his sonic blaster a squeeze. "*Aherk!*"

"Quiet!"

"You said no talking," Solly shrugged. "You didn't say no honking."

We went up through the door in the wall and into the light of day. It was chilly up so high in the mountains, and none of us had a jacket. The soldiers hurried us towards Kaspar Snit's mansion – up the circular stairs, and through the great front doors. Inside was a giant foyer with a marble floor, and overhead a chandelier made of thousands of glittering crystals.

"No lingering! This way."

We went down a long hallway. On either side stood elegant columns making little archways that my mother whispered to me were called porticoes. Even now, when our lives hung by a thread, she couldn't resist trying to teach me something. At the dining room entrance, two more soldiers stood at attention. One of them banged his pike on the ground and announced, "Your guests, O evil one."

"Show them in."

Kaspar Snit sat at the end of the longest dining table I had ever seen. It was covered in an exquisitely embroidered cloth and illuminated by the light from three candelabras along its length. Our four places were set at the other end, leaving a long empty space in the middle. The plates were of silver, the glasses crystal. On the walls around us were beautiful fresco paintings of birds and beasts and dancing gods and goddesses like I'd seen in my father's books on Italy.

"You ever thought of turning this place into a hotel?" I asked. "Of course you'd need to put in a swimming pool and cable television –"

"*Sit down!*" bellowed Kaspar Snit.

We sat down.

"That's better."

Five waiters entered from a hidden door, bringing in bowls of soup. Kaspar Snit sniffed the broth and smiled. "I hope you like turtle soup," he said.

"I hope you like a kick in the knee," Solly answered.

"Solly, that's really enough," my mother admonished him.

"Charming children," Kaspar Snit said, his upper lip curling. "I can see why couples are so anxious to have babies. Now tell me, Manfred, to what do I owe the unexpected pleasure of your visit?"

"As if you didn't know. You sent me those letters, Mr. Rapsak T. Ins."

"Clever name, don't you think?"

"And that cassette tape to Solly. Imagine, sending such a frightening message to a little boy."

"But I'm sure he enjoyed listening to it. And look at that outfit of his. I inspired him to be so creative. Don't parents like their children to use their imaginations?"

"And then there's what's right outside. The fountains you stole from Rome."

"And our fountain too," I said.

"How kind of you to notice my outdoor decorative touches. No doubt you brought that camera along, Manfred, to take some appreciative snapshots. But unfortunately we are like a museum here – we don't allow photographs to be taken."

"Have you got any postcards then?" Solly asked.

Kaspar Snit glared at him. "Guard!" he shouted. "Remove the camera!" In an instant the strap was lifted from around my father's neck and the camera taken away. Well, so much for part one of our plan.

My father said, "I must insist that you put all the fountains back."

"Oh, you insist? Then I suppose I'd better right away." A strange noise came from Kaspar Snit. It sounded like hiccups, and it made his Adam's apple bob up and down. It took me a moment to realize that he was laughing. "Yes, I'll put them all right back where I found them and then I'll write on the blackboard *I shall not steal any more fountains* one hundred times." Suddenly he stopped laughing and smacked his hand down on the table, making us all jump. "What do you take me for, Manfred? A not-very-nice person? A grouch? A meany? Don't you get it? I'm an *evil genius!* Evil geniuses don't give things back. They don't say 'I'm sorry.' Do the poor Romans miss their fountains? Well, too bad for them. They can live without beauty and so can the rest of the world. Those fountains will never be found. Are the Romans on the verge of going to war? Oh, goody. I love a big battle scene, don't you? Bombs blasting, buildings on fire, people running and screaming – now that's entertainment."

Kaspar Snit began his weird laugh again and just as abruptly stopped. "It appears as if none of you likes turtle soup. Such a shame – it was a very rare species of sea turtle, almost extinct." He clapped his hands and the waiters appeared with plates in their hands. They took our soup bowls and put down the plates.

"What is that?" Solly asked.

"Wild goats' brains. With just a hint of oregano. Trust me, you'll love it."

"Kaspar," my mother said. We all looked at her. She had used only his first name and with surprising softness. Kaspar Snit looked up at her too. My mother blushed but she didn't look away from him. "Kaspar, don't you remember our dinner in Rome all those years ago? We welcomed you like a member of the family. And after dinner we all stood on the balcony –"

"I *don't* want to talk about it!" he roared. "Lunch is over. Guards, take them away!"

"What?" said Solly, as a soldier lifted him out of his chair. "No dessert?"

16

AN

UNEXPECTED OFFER

The soldiers did not put us right back in the dungeon, but instead made us walk back and forth beside one of the inner walls of the fortress – an exercise period just as if we were convicts in a prison. We had to walk single file, separated from one another by a long space and with our eyes down so that we couldn't talk or send each other secret looks.

While we were walking, it was impossible not to notice another group of soldiers working nearby. They had some sort of contraption that they were pulling up alongside the first row of fountains, ten soldiers on each of the three ropes. The machine was as big as a tractor-trailer and had an odd, lumpy shape, hidden under a tarp. The soldiers heaved and groaned until finally they had it where they wanted. The next time I glanced up, I saw other soldiers coming with blowtorches, giant wrenches, and smaller tools as well. I was hoping they would take the tarp off, but instead they crawled underneath it. Soon I could hear screeches, whirs, hums, and hammering. On one of the turns to go the other way, my mother caught my eye. Her glance said: *What is that thing?*

"Keep your eyes down!" the captain barked. I did as commanded, staring at the dry earth under my feet. It was because my eyes were down that I noticed something peculiar – some small holes in the ground in a circle. On the next pass over, I brushed at the spot with my shoe, scraping off the dust and revealing iron. It was a grid, or manhole cover, set into the ground. And then I realized what it was – the iron grid over the window in the roof of the dungeon. It looked just about large enough for a kid my size to squeeze through.

On the next pass, I saw that the grid had a latch to keep it closed. I just had time to scuff it with my heel, moving it a little. The next time, I gave it a kick, dislodging the latch almost all the way. It needed just one more kick.

"Exercise period is over!" the captain shouted. "Back to the dungeon."

Oh no! I just couldn't go back before undoing that latch. Without thinking I bolted towards the grid. "Halt!" came the captain's cry, but I kept going. I stuck out my leg just as if I were sliding into home base and the side of my shoe hit the latch, pushing it open even as I tumbled head over heels.

Ouch. I lay on my stomach, face in the dust. When I tried to rise, I felt something sharp prod my back.

"Turn over."

I did as commanded. And saw a dozen soldiers, each with the blade end of his pike just inches from me.

"Try that again," the captain said, "and we'll put enough holes in you to become a fountain yourself. Understand?"

I was too scared to get any words out, so I just nodded.

"That was the most foolish, most reckless thing you have ever done, Eleanor. Trying to run away from the soldiers! Where could you even run? It's a good thing that none of them lost his head."

"I'm sorry, Dad," I said. "I just got scared, I guess."

"Well, that's understandable," my father said more gently. He came over to the straw where I was sitting and squeezed my shoulder. "But please be more careful. Let Mom and me figure out what to do. We'll get out of this somehow."

"All right."

"And now it's time to get some sleep," my mother said. "Lie down, Eleanor. You too, Solly."

We lay in the gloom of the dungeon. Our dinner had been stale bread and water, the classic prisoner's diet. First Mom and then Dad had given me long lectures about my trying to run, and since I didn't want to tell them about the grid, I just had to listen. I knew that if I did tell them, they would never let me try to do what I planned. It seemed to me that when it came to figuring out how we were going to get out of here, Mom and Dad needed some help. And the first step was to get back the amulet.

Solly snuggled up next to me. "Eleanor?" he said.

"Uh-huh?"

"I'm scared too."

"Are you, Solly? You don't sound it when you talk back to Kaspar Snit."

"Well, a superhero has to keep a stiff upper lip, doesn't he? Even if he is afraid."

"Anyway, we'll get out of this."

"Are you sure?"

"Yes, I'm sure. Now let's get some sleep."

"Okay, Eleanor."

I wasn't really sure at all, but there seemed no point in telling Solly that. It wasn't long before I could hear him whistling through his teeth as he breathed. My parents whispered to each other and then grew silent, but I waited some more to be sure that they were asleep. I got up, brushing off the straw, and took a few steps until I reached the dungeon wall. The good thing about dungeon walls being made out of stone is that the stone makes pretty good footholds for climbing. I hoisted myself up and kept going, one stone at a time, making sure I had good hand-holds as well.

About halfway up my foot slipped on a slippery stone, but I caught it on the next. A startled bat fluttered from the wall so that I had to stop myself from yelping in fright. More bats flew – the air became thick with them – but then they settled down again farther away. I kept going, stopping when I reached the ceiling, just beside the iron grate. The grate was rusty but a good push with the flat of my hand loosened it, and then I pushed it all the way off. I put one hand through and then the other, moved my foot to a higher stone on the wall, and pulled myself up through the hole.

And I was out. Now it was only a matter of finding our fountain, opening the secret compartment, and taking the amulet. That seemed easy enough, being alone on the grounds of the fortress, with only the stars above and the silvery shapes of the statues for company. But then my heart dropped as I heard voices. They were coming from the big tarp. I darted behind the nearest statue, a chubby cupid, so that I wouldn't be seen.

"A marvelous machine, don't you think, captain?" It was Kaspar Snit's deep, creepy voice.

"Yes, absolutely splendid, O evil one."

"I can't wait to see it work. It reminds me of when I was a young man, living in a single room. A mouse kept me up at night and so I bought a mousetrap. I stayed up all night. And then – *zing!* I have the same feeling now."

"I'm sure you will be very satisfied, your evil excellency."

"It must be ready by tomorrow."

"It will be. All it needs are some final adjustments and a cleaning of the intake tube. It would be done already if one of my privates hadn't thrown in the remains of his lunch, the imbecile."

"But I don't understand. This machine can turn marble into dust. How can a sandwich be a problem?"

"That's exactly why, your evil highness. It is made for hard substances. Marble. Rock. Concrete. It is not designed for anything soft. Fortunately, we turned the machine off in time. Just wait and see what it will do to those fountains."

"*Oooh*, I can't wait! I'm as excited as a child on his birthday. All right, captain. You are dismissed. Since this is the last night of existence for the fountains, I wish to spend a little time communing with them. Alone."

"Yes, my supreme evil leader."

"Oh, and captain, excellent use of names for me. Keep it up."

I heard the soldier's heavy boots as he walked towards the barracks. So the machine was for destroying the fountains. I couldn't believe that Kaspar Snit would do such an awful thing, yet that was clearly his intention. Now he started walking and I kept still as he passed, just on the other side of the cupid. I peeked out to see him strolling along, whistling under his breath and occasionally reaching out to stroke the smooth marble arm of one statue, the leg of another. Despite my parents' earlier warnings, I decided to follow him, dodging from one fountain to another but careful to keep behind. Kaspar Snit paused here and there to take a good last look before moving on. He made his way down to the corner of his fortress. And there he stopped.

It took me a moment to realize that the fountain he was standing in front of was ours. But there it was, the naked men and women on their horses, looking as if they were real living beings turned to stone by some magic spell. I must have been mesmerized by the sight of it – and of Kaspar Snit standing right next to the secret compartment – because I tripped on something in the dark, a broken piece of rock maybe, and banged my knee on the fountain I was hiding behind.

"*Ouch!*" I froze.

Kaspar Snit whirled around, his cape swirling behind him.

"Who's there?" he snarled.

I didn't answer, but just peaked out at him.

He put his hands out, forcing a narrow smile. "Don't be frightened, whoever you are. Come out and let me see you."

I hesitated another moment, but I knew that all Kaspar Snit had to do was call out and I would be surrounded by guards. So I stepped from my hiding place and stood facing him. His face registered surprise and then annoyance and then an extra dose of repugnance, as if he had a particular dislike for me. But he smiled again and said, "Ah, Eleanor, you are a clever one to find your way out of the dungeon."

He took a step towards me; I took a step back. He held up a hand, as if to say that he wouldn't come closer. "No doubt you are also admiring your father's fountain. It is quite a work, isn't it? What a shame it will have the same fate as the others. A shame for you and your annoying family, that is. For me, it will be pure fun."

"You know what? I think you're acting just like a spoiled little boy."

"*Oooh*," Kaspar Snit said, pretending to shiver. "Do you think you are hurting my feelings? Well, sticks and stones. . . ." The words faded out as an expression came over his face that made the corners of his mouth curl up. "I must say, Eleanor, you are a clever girl. I could use an assistant of my own, a sidekick. These soldiers of mine don't truly appreciate my originality. No, it would take a clever one like you to really grasp just how dastardly I can be." His voice growing enthusiastic now, he took a big step towards me. "What do you say, Eleanor? How about kissing that family of yours good-bye and coming to join me? Just think how much fun we'd have together! The two of us could get up to no end of no good. And we'd be famous too. That's right, the evil Kaspar Snit and his notorious sidekick, Eleanor. You could even wear a black cape like mine, although maybe with a little silver trim to give it a feminine touch. Yes, that's just what I've been missing. I must say, I'm an even greater genius than I myself knew. So what do you say? Do you agree?"

He had moved so close to me that I could smell his sour breath. His eyes shone with nasty hopefulness. I wished that I could think of something clever to say, but I was too scared. Finally I managed to squeak out a few words: "I'd like to go back to the dungeon now. To my family."

His eyes narrowed. The expectant smile on his face turned downward. With his big hand he grabbed me by the back of my shirt collar and, lifting me off the ground, carried me swiftly between the dark fountains.

"Refuse a generous offer from me, will you? Well, that's

the last one you'll get, I assure you. Yes, go and join your revolting family – at least while you can. Because tomorrow will be the end of you all!"

We had reached the open grate, which Kaspar Snit must have seen as he was hauling me along, because now he held me right over it, grinning in the most hideous manner. And then he let go.

17

INTERVIEW
WITH THE EVIL ONE

It was a good thing that straw was heaped on the dungeon floor, but even so I landed with a pretty hard *womp*. Solly stirred but he didn't wake up, and I curled up to him, glad for the company, and fell into a deep sleep.

In the morning the arrival of the captain with breakfast woke us up. My body felt sore all over. Solly looked at the cold gruel in his chipped bowl and reluctantly picked up the wooden spoon and put it in his mouth. "This is awful," he said. "It tastes like the paste we use in school."

"How do you know what paste tastes like?" I asked, trying to swallow the stuff.

"Because I tried it once. Doesn't everybody?"

"Solly," Mom said, "when we get home again, there will be no more eating of school supplies."

"*If* we get home again," Solly said.

"I'm sure we will."

My father was still lying on his back, his bowl of gruel untouched. "Solly's right," he said. "We might as well stop kidding ourselves. There's no way out of here."

"Manfred, we need to be optimistic for the children."

"Maybe it's better to be realistic."

The captain came for the bowls and I gathered them up. Solly said to him, "So what do *you* get for breakfast?"

"The same thing," said the captain. "Only two helpings."

"Ever think of going into another line of work?"

"Actually," the captain said, "I wanted to be a ballet dancer."

The four of us couldn't help turning our heads. Mom said, "Why didn't you?"

"Poor turnout." He demonstrated by putting his feet, in their big boots, in first position. His toes didn't turn outward as much as they were supposed to.

"Maybe you just need to practise," Solly said.

"That's what I hoped. Then I got captured by Kaspar Snit and forced into his army. But once a year, the soldiers have a talent night. We're not supposed to, but I say, what the evil one doesn't know won't hurt him. We've got some real talent in the ranks. But I'm not allowed to fraternize with you." He put on his mean guard's voice. "Give me those bowls right away!"

I brought them to the guard. Rising on my tiptoes to be closer to his ear, I whispered, "I want to see Kaspar Snit. Alone. Can you ask him?"

"I don't know. I might get into trouble."

"If you don't, I'll tell Kaspar Snit about the talent night."

"You wouldn't!"

"Okay, I wouldn't. But can't you ask him? I know, tell him that I'm considering his offer. He'll understand."

"All right. I just hope I won't regret it."

I hadn't intended to try and see Kaspar Snit again, but while we were talking to the captain an idea had come to me. For the next hour there was nothing to do, so Solly and I played X's and O's by scratching with a stone on the dungeon wall. Beating Solly was too easy because he hadn't yet figured out that the best place to put your first X was the center, and I had to pretend not to see what he was doing so that he could win once in a while. Then the soldiers returned to take us out for the exercise period, and once more we went up the long stairway into the sunlight.

Kaspar Snit's marble-crushing machine was still there, only now the tarp had been removed. It looked even bigger than before, as long as a bus. At one end, a conveyer belt led into the intake tube, which looked like the wide end of a vacuum cleaner. Then came all kinds of gears and switches, a series of hammerlike things that looked as if they could swing up and down, a bellows, a pair of wings (at least they looked like wings), a thin glass tube with markings on it that looked like a giant thermometer. At the other end, a fat hose rose up and then twisted back down, ending a few feet short of the ground. Only two soldiers were working on it now – one tightening screws and the other polishing the metal.

"Whatever it is," my father said, "it doesn't look good."

I didn't have the heart to tell him, and besides, one of the soldiers growled at us to keep quiet and we started our forced trek to nowhere. We were on our third trip when a voice cried, "Halt!" and I looked up to see the captain who wanted to be a dancer standing with his pike planted on the earth.

"That one," he said pointing to me. "You must come."

"Why?" said my mother anxiously. "She didn't do anything."

"I said come."

I took a step forward, and so did my mother. "I'll come too," she said.

"No," the captain said fiercely. "Just her. Now march!"

And so I went, the captain so close behind me that the wooden pike brushed against my back. He said in a low voice, "Sorry for sounding that way. Got to do the job, you know. He'll see you."

"Thanks."

The captain led me to the mansion and into the foyer. I remembered how it felt when he had lifted me up by my shirt collar, and suddenly my idea didn't seem like such a good one. We took a different hallway this time, leading to the library. The room was completely round, with a domed ceiling, and it was lined with bookshelves right up to the very top. At first I didn't realize that Kaspar Snit himself was sitting, his back to the door, at an ornate desk that stood on a round Persian rug. The captain knocked his pike on the floor.

"The girl, O evil entity."

"All right," Kaspar Snit said, his back still to me. "You may go."

The captain looked as if he wanted to whisper something, but then thought better of it and left, closing the door behind him. I was more scared than when I had seen Kaspar Snit by the fountain the night before, maybe because I had time to think about it. I could feel my knees trembling so much that they knocked together. Slowly he turned around. He wore his black cape as always, and his pointed beard looked as if it had just been trimmed. He gazed at me with his small black eyes.

"Approach," he said.

I took a hesitant step forward.

"Closer."

I came right up to the desk. Kaspar stared at me hard and I tried to stare back, looking into the glassy depths of those eyes.

"So you have changed your mind, have you?"

"I beg your pardon?"

"You want to join me after all."

"Oh, no, that's a little misunderstanding. I'm here because . . . well . . . because I want to help you."

One dark eyebrow went up. "You want to help *me*?"

"Yes, Mr. Snit, I do. You see, I've been thinking about it and I don't believe you are really evil."

His voice grew a notch more menacing. "You don't?"

"No, I don't. Not a hundred percent, anyway. You just

want your soldiers to call you evil one and evil highness to convince yourself that you are. Oh, you've done a lot of bad things; I've no doubt about that. And there's a lot of bad feeling in you. But there's something else, too. Maybe it isn't very big, maybe it's only a tiny spot in your heart, but it's there. That's why you got so mad at us all those years ago when you came to dinner in Rome. That's why you got mad at me for calling you nice. Because you thought it might be true. And it scared you because you're so used to being bad. So you protected yourself by deciding to hate us. But, if you wanted, you could go the other way. I'm sure of it. Instead of squashing that little spot in your heart, you could let it grow bigger. I bet it could grow so big that it would become the big part of your heart and the evil become the little speck. I just know it. And you know what? Then you would enjoy the good things. Like grass and trees and birds. And parks and violins and fountains. And you could feel differently about people too. You could like them and people would like you back. . . ."

Talking so much, my voice had grown not louder but softer. Kaspar Snit was breathing hard, like maybe he was going to cry. He brushed his hand over one eye and then a tear, a real tear, did squeeze out of that little dark eye and roll down his gaunt cheek.

"Do you really think it's not too late?"

"Yes, I do," I said excitedly. "And you know how you can start? By making a friend. Me."

"You would be my . . . my friend?"

"Sure I would."

At that moment two loud cracks came from the doorway. It was the captain, banging his pike on the floor. "Your magnificent evilness, the machine is now ready. The soldiers are in formation and the Blande family is being held outside. We only need your signal to begin."

Kaspar Snit waited a moment. And then he smiled the most cruel smile I have ever seen. He opened his hand and showed me a small tube. "Glycerin drops," he said. "They look like real tears. Did I fool you, dear little Eleanor? Well, you're wrong. It *is* too late." He stood up, flourishing his cape. "All right, captain," he said, his voice deepening. "Take the girl and let's go."

18

THE SNIT MARBLE-CRUSHING MACHINE

Kaspar Snit came outside first, while the captain and I followed. As soon as they saw their leader, the soldiers snapped to attention and pounded their pikes against the ground. Beside the machine a giant forklift truck idled, holding our own fountain. And the amulet hidden inside it. Mom and Dad and Solly, with soldiers on either side of them, anxiously waited for me to join them. As soon as I got there they hugged me, Solly grabbing me around the legs so that I almost toppled over.

"Are you all right, Eleanor?" Mom asked. "What were you doing in there?"

"Quiet!" shouted the captain. "The great Kaspar Snit, most evil of all evildoers, is about to speak."

Silence. Kaspar Snit bowed in acknowledgment. "Today," he said, "we are at a most historic event, my first act of evil on a truly monumental scale. And it is only the beginning, for wherever people are enjoying themselves, there is work to be done. I think it is only fitting that our intruders are here to witness this moment. How much sweeter it will be for me to watch your face, Manfred, as those fountains enter the crushing machine one by one. I have even found a way to use those fountains to increase my already sizeable fortune. You see, I will turn all that fine Italian marble into gravel for fish tanks."

"You wouldn't!" said my father.

"Wouldn't I? Let me demonstrate. As you can see, we have installed a conveyer belt leading to the intake tube of the crushing machine. My soldiers will now put in a sample. Start the machine!"

So the rat really had been faking those tears. I turned and saw on the conveyer belt a large marble head that must have come from an ancient statue. A soldier standing at the ready used two hands to pull an enormous switch. Immediately the siren wailed, then came a series of chugs as steam pumped forth from a metal chimney, then the whirring of gears, the flapping of wings, and the sudden jerking forward of the marble head as the conveyer belt started to move. The head entered the big jaw of the intake tube, hesitated a moment, then lurched inside. An awful grinding sound began and then the hammerlike devices attached to the machine began to pound up and down with such force that the ground shook beneath our feet.

The white smoke from the chimney turned to gray and then black, whistles blew, the wings thumped faster, and the red line in the tube that looked like a thermometer began to rise. The down tube started shaking as if it would burst. A rattle of gravel poured from it into a plastic bag held beneath by a metal hoop. The bag filled and then was automatically sealed, labeled, and spat onto the ground. Another and another followed. More than twenty bags of gravel were packaged before the machine came to a wheezing halt. The soldier yanked up the switch.

Kaspar Snit picked up a bag and threw it at us. My father caught it and we all looked at the label. It showed a drawing of a smiling Kaspar Snit, holding a goldfish up by the tail. Under him were the words SNIT'S PREMIUM AQUARIUM GRAVEL.

"*Ugh*," said Solly. "The picture looks just like you."

"At five dollars a bag," Kaspar Snit said, "I'll make millions."

"You'll never get away with this," Dad said. "Somehow justice will be done and you'll be punished."

"It will?" Kaspar Snit said, and rubbed at his beard, pretending to think. "*Mmm*, I'd better do something about that. I know! How about we wait until there is only one fountain left and then put you and your picture-perfect family under the outtake tube of my crushing machine? Then we'll place the fountain on the conveyer belt and bury you in gravel. What a gloriously nasty idea!"

My father took a step forward. Two soldiers clanged their pikes together to stop him from going farther. "Please,

Mr. Snit," he said. "You can't do that to my children. If you would let them go at least, and Daisy too, then I could stay and . . . and help you in your plans."

"No," said my mother. "Let me stay."

"How touching. A last minute plea from a desperate father and mother. Your willingness to sacrifice yourselves is most endearing. But I'm not in the mood. Now, enough talk. It's time for action. Soldiers, are you ready?"

"Yes, O evil one!" they said in unison.

"Then put in the Blandes' fountain!"

Kaspar Snit clapped his hands twice. The soldiers parted and the forklift truck raised our fountain higher. It trundled forward and heaved the fountain onto the conveyer belt. The captain himself pulled down the switch and once more the siren wailed, smoke puffed from the chimney, gears whirred, wings flapped. The fountain moved along the conveyer belt towards the jaws of the intake tube.

I looked at my father and saw his stricken face. Oh, if only I could do something!

"Wait!" I called. "Just let me say good-bye to our fountain."

"How nauseatingly sentimental," said Kaspar Snit. But he didn't stop me as I ran up to the conveyer belt and put my hands on the fountain as if I were hugging it. With my right hand I pressed against the secret door and, as it opened, I grasped hold of the amulet and quickly shut it again, hoping that nobody could see.

"Get back in place!" Kaspar Snit commanded. I hurried

over to my parents and Mom put her arm around my shoulder while I pressed the amulet into my palm. Then I slipped it in my pocket.

"I guess this isn't a job for Googoo-man after all," Solly said morosely.

"Maybe it is, Solly," I whispered. "Have you got your sock? I mean, your neutronic knocker?"

"Sure, it's on the other side, here in my belt."

"What's in it anyway?"

"Bubble gum."

"Bubble gum?"

"Every day I chewed a piece of bubble gum and then put it in. Took me weeks to fill it."

"That's disgusting," I said. But I was thinking. *Bubble gum: soft, sticky, gooey.*

"Quick, Solly! Throw the neutronic knocker into the machine."

"Why?"

"Just do it. And don't miss!"

"If you say so."

He had some trouble pulling it from his belt, but then he wound up his arm and tossed the neutronic knocker in the air. He threw it so high, I thought it would never land in the right spot. The two of us watched as it began to descend and landed on the conveyer belt just inches in front of the fountain. It disappeared inside and a low moan came from the machine. It shuddered. The conveyer belt jerked backwards, forwards, and backwards again.

"What is going on?" Kaspar Snit said.

"I'm sure everything's fine, O Olympic medalist of evil," the captain said.

But it wasn't fine. The conveyer belt shuddered to a halt, with the fountain just an inch from the jaws. The machine began to cough, burp, and bang, and then it started shaking crazily. The wings flapped harder and harder until one broke off. The red line in the glass tube was going up and up. The white smoke turned to pink.

"Pink smoke?" said Dad.

"Bubble gum," nodded Solly.

"Oh, my . . ." said Mom, for the noises coming from the crushing machine had grown louder. It was shaking so hard that parts were flinging everywhere and we had to duck. And then something began to emerge from the chimney.

"Look!" Dad gasped in amazement. "It's . . . it's. . . ."

"A bubble," I said.

It *was* a bubble, pink and round. The bubble grew larger and larger as it emerged from the top of the chimney until it was as big as a hot air balloon.

Kaspar Snit cried, "Something's wrong! Turn off the machine!"

"I can't," said the captain. "The switch won't budge. The works are all gummed up."

"Bubble-gummed up, actually," said Solly.

"GET DOWN!" yelled my father. "It's going to blow!"

I dropped to my knees and covered my head with my hands. There was a tremendous *BOOM!* And then the sound of ripping metal. Something was falling on my head – stringy bits of bubble gum. *Yuck.*

"My beautiful machine!" screamed Kaspar Snit. "Curse you, Manfred Blande, and your sniveling children. Just wait and see what I'll do to you!"

"Solly," I said, "Give me the end of your superelastic belt."

"Okay," he said, not questioning me this time. I took it in one hand and put my hands in position. Then I tilted up my chin and closed my eyes. If ever there was a time I needed to think *fly*, it was now.

"Eleanor!" Mom said. She must have noticed my position. "What are you doing?" But I didn't wait. I rose into the air and hovered some twenty feet up. I could hear the gasps of the soldiers and even of Kaspar Snit as they noticed me.

"What's this?" Kaspar cried. "A girl who *flies*?"

I paid no attention, but instead flew round and round Solly to unravel the superelastic belt. When it was free, I rose higher and dangled the end of it right in front of Kaspar Snit's nose.

"Hey, Uncle Kaspy," I sang, "would you mind holding the end of this for a minute?"

"How can you fly? I must know! I must!" Kaspar growled. But he grabbed the end just as I'd asked him. Maybe he thought he could pull me down. Immediately I began to fly in tight circles around him, wrapping his black-clad figure in elastic. Afraid to get hit by a flying girl, the soldiers backed away. Within a moment, I had Kaspar Snit's arms and legs pinned. I landed again – not so gracefully, I have to admit – and Mom finished the job by tying a knot.

"Get me out of this!" Kaspar Snit demanded.

"I'm afraid not," my father said. "At least not until those fountains are returned to Rome."

"You've forgotten one thing," Kaspar Snit said, and slowly grinned. "My army. Captain! Take hold of the Blandes and get me loose!"

Of course. How foolish of us to have forgotten the soldiers. "It was a good try," Mom said, pulling Solly and me towards her.

But the soldiers didn't move. "What are you waiting for?" Kaspar Snit bellowed. "Cut me out of this ridiculous elastic straitjacket. And then use your blades on the Blandes. Poke them more full of holes than a spaghetti strainer!"

The captain barked out an order and the soldiers raised their pikes. My father stepped forward, holding out his hands. "Now listen, fellas," he said. "I'm sure all this can be settled peacefully. If you would just look at matters a different way –"

The captain interrupted him. "You have tied up the evil one!"

"I don't know if I'd use the word 'tied' exactly. . . ."

"Three cheers, men. *Hip hip hooray!* Three cheers for Eleanor! *Hip hip hooray!*"

The soldiers cheered, throwing their helmets into the air so that we had to duck in order not to be clobbered by them. A moment later they were swarming around us, patting us on our backs and shaking our hands.

"Are we ever glad," the captain said. "That Kaspar Snit is a nasty piece of work."

"Yes," said another soldier. "If we hadn't been so afraid of him, we'd have tied him up ourselves. Come on, then, you must be famished. Let's open up the storehouse! Bring food and drink! It's time to celebrate! And after that, we'll start taking the fountains back to Rome."

"Oh, thank goodness," my father said with relief.

"Have you forgotten about me?" Kaspar Snit snarled, struggling uselessly in his bonds.

"Be quiet, you," said the captain. "We've had enough of your evil genius for one day."

19

THE GREAT
FOUNTAIN AIRLIFT

One hour later, we began to take back the fountains. Kaspar Snit's former soldiers started up the helicopters, attached the chains, and before long we were flying in formation. It took six helicopters to raise the Trevi Fountain, three for the Leaky Boat, and one to carry the Porter. The soldiers, glad to be free, all agreed to keep my flying a secret, and Mom and Dad and Solly and I rode in the helicopters too. Mom, however, made sure to take the amulet back from me and put it around her neck.

It took several hours to get to the shore of Italy, by which time we had already been spotted flying over several other countries. Also, the captain had radioed our approach to the Italian air traffic control. He told them that the fountains had not been stolen by another country, but by

Kaspar Snit, and that we were now on our way to return them. The news must have made it immediately to Italian television and radio because the streets of the first town we flew over was crowded with people cheering and waving at us from below.

By the time we got to Rome, the entire city was waiting. I was in one of the helicopters carrying the Trevi Fountain and, as we lowered it back into place, a roar rose up from the people, so loud that it drowned out the noise of the helicopters. As soon as we landed, people rushed towards us. A woman I had never seen before gave me a big hug, and then she and some others lifted me onto their shoulders. Mom, Dad, and Solly too got lifted up, and the four of us were marched triumphantly up the famous street called the Corso. I smiled and waved to the crowd all around us and Solly, wearing his Googoo-man costume, looked over and gave me a thumbs-up sign.

The crowd carried us all the way to the steps of the City Hall, where the mayor of Rome waited for us along with a delegation of important-looking people wearing medals and ribbons. Four little girls in white dresses came forward to give us enormous bouquets of roses, and then the mayor handed each of us a giant key to the city and named us all honorary citizens of Rome.

"The people of Rome thank the Blande family," the mayor boomed into the microphone as the crowd cheered again. "They have returned our precious fountains to us. The government of Italy has taken its army off the alert. The threat of war is over and the true perpetrator of this crime, Kaspar Snit, will be punished. But now is a time to rejoice. To dance in the streets! Let us celebrate!"

And so we did. That evening there was a banquet in a palace, with singers and dancers and more food than I had ever seen before. Solly and I were allowed to stay up late and, at the stroke of midnight, the mayor himself took us out onto the balcony of the palace to watch a display of fireworks over the Tiber River.

Mom, Dad, Solly, and I were given another, smaller palace to stay in. I was so excited that I thought I would never be able to fall asleep, so I just looked up at the beautiful angels painted on the ceiling above the four-poster bed. Mom and Dad came in together to say good night.

"We're very proud of you and Solly," my father said, kissing my forehead. "You were smart and you were brave."

"And a good flyer," my mother whispered, kissing me too.

I must have fallen asleep shortly after because I could not remember anything else until I awoke to the sound of birds outside the window.

It took twelve more days for the helicopters to return all the fountains to where they belonged – THE GREAT FOUNTAIN AIRLIFT all the newspapers called it. In the meantime, we toured the city, recognized and applauded wherever we went. People came up to give us necklaces of flowers, while all the restaurant owners urged us to let them treat us to a gourmet meal. No one, they said, had ever seen Rome like this before.

After all the fountains had been returned, it took another week for the plumbers of Rome to reattach them to the pipes that brought water from the aqueducts. When they were done, the mayor declared a national holiday. He picked us up in a white limousine and we drove through the city, which was festooned with flowers, streamers, and balloons. A special place had been reserved for us just in front of the huge basin of the Trevi Fountain, where we stood with a crowd behind us, waiting for the marble to come alive again. "See?" my father said, and smiled. "If you throw a coin in the Trevi Fountain, you always come back." And then, at the tolling of the noon bells, the water was turned on. It flowed, poured, sprayed, gushed, gurgled, streamed, and cascaded.

For a long moment, all the people who had come out to witness the event remained silent with the pleasure of it. Then a great cheer went up and the crowd began to laugh and sing. They brought out mandolins and guitars and accordions and, as people began to play, women and men and children kicked up their heels. They reached out to me and Solly and Mom and Dad and soon we were in the middle of it all, and never did I have so much fun.

There was only one sour face in all of Rome and it belonged to Kaspar Snit. The captain had brought him to the city in a helicopter and he was taken to the central jail. He was going to be charged with theft, damage to public property, inciting war, and many other offences. I wondered if I was the only one who felt just a little sorry for him.

And so we returned home, this time taking an airplane courtesy of the Italian government. We didn't talk much on the plane ride; I think we were all too tired and full of everything that had happened. We took a taxicab from the airport to our house. It had been great to see Rome, but I couldn't wait to be home again.

In the taxi, Solly kept falling asleep, his head nodding onto my shoulder, and I kept tilting him the other way. Finally we pulled up to the house and I opened the car door with relief. What did I see but our very own fountain rising up in front of our house. Mom and Dad and Solly came up beside me and we stood watching the jets of water rise from the conch shells and tumble down the eight naked men and women and their horses. Someone had tied a red ribbon around the neck of every figure. And leaning against the basin was a little hand-lettered sign:

WE ARE GLAD TO HAVE "OUR" FOUNTAIN BACK
YOUR NEIGHBORS

"Well," Dad said. "Isn't that nice."

All would have been perfect if my father had not received an E-mail from Italy the very next morning. We were just sitting down to breakfast when he came into the kitchen, absorbed in reading the sheet of paper in his hand.

"Please don't tell us that a fountain is missing," Mom said.

"No," said Dad, without looking up. "But Kaspar Snit is."

"What?" all three of us said at once.

"He picked the lock of his jail cell. Seems as if that was one of the talents he had learned in his criminal youth. Then he went to the roof of the prison, where several dozen helium balloons from the celebrations had become caught in some wires. Kaspar Snit used them to float off the roof. He was last seen drifting away."

"But he couldn't have gone far with a handful of balloons," Mom said.

"Well, he hasn't been seen since. The police in seven countries are looking for him. Why is it that I doubt they'll find him?"

"Oh, well," Mom said. "I'm sure he'll never cause trouble again."

"He also left a note," Dad said, looking at the E-mail again. "I'll read it to you."

This is not the last that you will hear of the evil Kaspar Snit. And the next time that I fly, it will not be with balloons.

My father looked at me. "He wants to know how to fly, Eleanor."

"*Oops*," I said. And then, "I'm sure he's just bluffing, Dad. I bet he's learned not to mess with the Blande family."

"I hope you're right."

"Hey, Mom, where did you put the amulet anyway? I did happen to notice that it's not in the secret compartment of the fountain anymore."

"I think I'll keep that little secret to myself."

Dad crumpled up the E-mail and threw it into the garbage can under the sink. He said, "I've forgotten to turn on the fountain. I guess I'm out of the habit. I don't suppose anyone wants to come out with me."

"I'll come," said Solly.

"Me too," said Mom.

"Make that three," I said.

We trooped outside and lined up on the sidewalk. It was funny, but I didn't feel embarrassed by the fountain anymore. Dad opened the little door and turned the tap and we all watched the jets of water rise up from the conch shells and splash down into the basin. I was about to follow Solly back inside when I felt a tap on my shoulder and turned to see Julia Worthington beside me. She wasn't in her gymnastics outfit this time, just regular clothes.

"Hi, Eleanor," she said.

"Hi, Julia."

"I'm glad the fountain is back. Even my dad is glad. He's the one who wrote that sign."

"I thought maybe he was."

Julia looked like she wanted to say something to me. She looked at me and then down at her feet, scuffing one running shoe against the other. For a moment I had the urge once again to tell her that I could fly, but it wasn't so strong and it didn't last more than a moment. It was funny, but I suddenly felt that if there really was anything special about me, it wasn't that I could fly. Maybe it was that I could be scared but also brave and smart, at least some of the time. And that I tried to see the good in people, even if they didn't always see it in themselves.

Julia looked up again and smiled awkwardly.

"I quit gymnastics," she said.

"You did? Why? You're so good at it. You always win medals."

"I know, but I just don't like it anymore. I guess I got tired of competing and trying to be the best at everything. Maybe I'll take up something else instead, something just for fun. My parents weren't too thrilled at first, but now they're okay about it."

"Do you still play the harp?"

"Oh, sure, I still like the harp."

"So that's good. I'd like to learn to play the guitar. An electric guitar, I mean."

"You would? That's a great idea. . . ."

We talked for a few more minutes and even agreed that it might be fun to do our homework together sometimes. I went back into the house feeling good. Mom and Dad and Solly were all hanging around the living room and Dad was tuning his mandolin.

"Since we're talking about flying . . ." Solly began.

"Who's talking about flying?" said Dad.

"We were before." Solly was sitting upside down in an overstuffed reclining chair. "So where are we going to fly to next?"

The three of us looked at him. My father answered rather sternly, "I think the flying days for this family are over."

Mom continued to work on the crossword puzzle in the newspaper. "You know, Manny," she said, in her most soothing voice, "the children do have a natural talent for it. It's nice to see they've inherited something from me. I'm sure if they were strictly supervised –"

Before she could finish, Solly and I had jumped out of our chairs to throw our arms around Dad. What else could he do but sigh with resignation? Mom asked him to play something on his mandolin and he started up a happy, quick-tempo tune that had us dancing around the room like we had done in Rome. When we were all so tired that we had to stop, we fell onto the chairs and sofas. Through the open windows of the house, I could hear the splash and play of falling water from the fountain outside. I thought that it was the most beautiful sound I had ever heard.

Acknowledgments

I wish to thank my brother, Lawrence Fagan, for letting me tag along on one of his trips to Italy. Thanks also to Kathy Lowinger and Sue Tate for their editorial acumen. Rachel and Sophie Fagan continue to be my most appreciative – and toughest – critics. H.V. Morton's elegant book, *The Fountains of Rome*, published in 1966, was both a help and an inspiration. Finally, my gratitude to the Ontario Arts Council for financial support.